MW00954508

Story of Stories

Dedication

This book is dedicated to Erica. Her strength, loving and kind heart, matched by her beautiful smile and zest for life are, and always will be, unprecedented ....

Thank you to all her family and friends that were there for her through life and beyond ...

Miss Ladu's writer's notebook Dedication (2012)

I dedicate this book to my mother who has always encouraged me to try my hardest and never fear failure. I love her very much and I know that I am a better person because of her love, guidance, and support.

Miss Ladu's writer's notebook Dedication (no date)

"It's not what you look at that matters, it's what you see." -Henry David Thoreau

I dedicate this notebook to my mom. She was the first one to see the writer in me, and has always encouraged me to do my best.

I also dedicate this book to my grandmother, who spent hours at the library with me and made me learn to appreciate the beauty of words.

Introduction

This is a story of stories by a young girl who dedicated her life to educating children and people on all things important to her. One of her life dreams was to one day be published, so in honor of that wish we have compiled all her writings and thoughts to share her short journey.

The person that wrote the stories is Erica Lynn and the person that finished her work is her mom. Erica has a double master in English and Literature, and was practicing for that one BIG idea that was going to launch her writing. Some of her stories were not completed and that is where her mom steps in to help finish some and leave the rest for the imagination of the reader, hopefully that's how Erica would have wanted it. Not all of the writings were dated but I know they were all within the last ten years.

The book is broken down into two parts; the first part are *Stories* that she started to write, poems, short stories, and lyric's. Some were complete, some were not and some could not be finished as they were only a start of something bigger. You will find that she had a vast imagination and lust of beauty indoors and out.

The second part of the book are some of her *Life Experiences*. Some are very personal stories or journeys

– I'm not even sure she would want them included but I think they will remind those of us who knew her how she felt sometimes.

The journals and notebooks that were used ranged from 2006 to 2016, she loved to write and was always jotting down her ideas. If anyone wants to finish an unfinished story – she would be happy someone shared the same idea with her and I would love to read it!

I hope you enjoy our stories as we walk you through Erica's thoughts and journey.

"What wound did ever heal but by degrees?"

-William Shakespeare (Othello)

Death leaves a heartache no one can heal, love leaves a memory no one can steal.

Stories

There is a small speck of gray
That rests on the crest of her eye
Washed to a shade of lilac
But only when she cries.

When she looks out at the sun
They turn toward a shade of blue
She is a gifted beautiful soul
Only one of a very few.

Her voice carries over the trees
Across the water through the windows
On the heels of eagles
In the tailwinds of dark crows.

Her face is still and pale
A shade of peach flushed in pink
And from gazing upon her features,
One would never think.

That this beauty is gracefully still
In a world that is not ours
Her glow, her sound and smile
Will always shine down from the stars.

-Erica Lynn

Airline Story

Cassandra did her job on trips like these. True, she held a coveted position as a flight attendant on one the most luxurious and overpriced airlines available. But this high-end lifestyle came with some high-end attitudes and these attitudes tended to flare up with jet stream power when poised at 30K for too long. 17 hours, the trip from New York to Japan was just such. But she had student loans to pay, and very little could compare to the money available as a Virgin Air hostess. So, as she walked the gangway, toward the dim tunnel and black hole, she felt the sense of underwhelmed anxiety pull at her. She dropped her purse and forced the square box luggage, that became her life, into the overhead compartment. Reaching over some pre-boarded 1st class guests, she slammed the compartment shut and turned to return to the front. But before she had made it an aisle away, she heard the dreaded click, bang and gasp.

"Sir! Oh my God! Are you okay?!" Her over-stuffed bag had succeeded in imploding, forcing the overhead door open and toppling its contents onto the unsuspecting guest. The man dug himself from beneath a wall of clothes and looked up at Cassandra. With his brow frowned poised to tear her a new one, he froze. Never in his life had he seen such single beauty, original elegance in one girl before. He was captivated in awe and lost in the softness of her blue eyes. "Sir? Please, I'm so sorry, are you ok?!" She pled as she assembled her bras and panties, now dangling from his shoulders. "No, yeah, really, I'm fine. Please stop fussing."

Cassandra piled everything in a pile behind the worn-out zipper and scurried away. If this is the worst thing that happens on this flight, I'll be happy!

*****

12/19/15

The hills billowed with steam - the warmth of the land turning the damp winter air into a sky of gray. The edges of the hills blurred into the pale ceiling of the clouds. The news warned of torrential downpours later this afternoon, but that would never stop Mr. Willonghly from making his weekly trip to the sea. And it certainly wasn't enough to stop my weekly trip to see Mr. Willonghly see the sea.

But something wasn't quite right today. Perhaps it was the ominous sky overhead. Perhaps it was the stillness of the sea, in sharp contrast with the turbulent skies. Or perhaps it was the fact that this was the first Sunday in 44 Sundays that Mr. Willonghly wasn't seeing the sea.

It was now 8:17, 12 minutes after Mr. Willonghly should have taken his first steps onto the sand, 7 minutes after his elderly gait should have brought him to the edge of the tide, and 6 minutes after he should have removed his cap, and nodded his reverence to the whisking waves.

My heart was heavy with the unknown. I waited a little longer and accepted the fact that Mr. Willonghly will not be enjoying the sea as he did each week. I stood with my face to the direction of the wind off the water, at the point of lands end and where the ocean begins, I look to the memory of the ones gone before me, the light and the meaning of the voices on the wind.

(finished story from "voices on the wind" – Little Feat)

Lyric Poem #1

This assignment is awful
Fills me with fear
What if I stutter
Will everyone hear?

I'm going to mess up
Forget a few lines
Stumble on words
Mess up a few rhymes

What if I faint?
Completely pass out?
It's likely to happen
Without a doubt.

But what if I don't
And do really well
Through my recitation
A story I'll tell.

Find a new talent.
A new way to express
All that I feel
My new-found prowess

Maybe I'll turn into
A famous new writer
My audience will demand more
With the flicker of lighters

I'll travel the world
And cross tepid seas
All because Miss Ladu
Inspired me.

*****

"The pain passes but the beauty remains"

-Pierre Auguste Renoir

Lyric Poem

I open the door
The heat fills the room
I can't breathe
The dampness consumes

My every breathe
And desperate gasp
Trying to focus
But losing my grasp

I don't want to work
Any more than you do
But I am here suffering
Right next to you

Please try to focus
On why we were here
263 days left
Till you're in the clear

Ignore the dampness
The sweat on your brow
Enjoy the fun.
Stay with me now.

*****

"What we have once enjoyed and deeply loved we can never lose, for all that we love deeply becomes part of us"   -Helen Keller

Haden stretched her legs out, past the sill of the window, her toes meeting the bit of November air. The leaves had now fallen and the tree limbs now poke the gray skies that seemed to hang low in the forest.

The snow would start soon, it always came by Thanksgiving. The ride to Aunt Carrie's house in the mountains was always lined with that dirt-smeared slush, scraped up with the salt and sand, dropped to gain traction. Too bad it wasn't enough to keep all cars on the road.

She snapped herself out of her stream of consciousness, aware of how much she would regret starting her day this way, and sat upright. Though she was just of average height, she felt like a giant in the cramped barn loft. She had to crawl on hands and knees just to reach the makeshift ladder in the corner. This was undoubtedly not what the structure was made for.

Though it was old and falling apart, the glass long gone from the windows and shingles wind torn from the roof, even in its earliest days, it seemed to be quite inhospitable, even for the simplest of person. It certainly wasn't the cozy colonial with a white picket fence and blue shutters Haden had known most of her life.

Letting her legs dangle off the edge of the loft, she pulled her hair into a knot and secured it with a pink elastic. It was the only one she brought, not having stopped to consider her hair amidst the chaos. These things tended to stretch out after several wearing's, before being rendered useless, just another piece of fabric, purpose abated, discarded into the trash, left to nothingness besides the rotting banana peels and used paper towels.

Photo prompt #1

The swirls of the tents spun around and around, twisting and turning in the hypnotic rhythm, pulling me into a trance – fooling me into a false slumber. Outside I could hear the swoosh of the Ferris wheel as it made its full rotation. There was a loose cart that was never quite right. I could count the full rotation by the approach and pass of the cart, it's safety chain planking against the frame. It wasn't even attached half the time. The cart swing too freely, then the hook just released. Some "safety" chain! If people only knew how haphazardly these rides were put together. I mean, who could blame us? 48 fairs a year, 26 states. That meant unloading, arranging, assembling, operating, disassembling, rearranging, reloading and moving these giant pieces of equipment 48 times. It became almost like a robotic habit. He didn't even really need to pay attention to what we were doing. Most of the time, the bolts were put where they belonged. Most of the time, the safety chains were connected. Most of the time, our patrons were safe. Most of the time.

I was just off a 26-hour shift. Truly, the 3 feet tall groundskeeper had come down with a stomach bug and refused to come out of his tent. Claimed it felt like rabid squirrels were trying to escape from his belly button. Although I'm fairly certain that it was a pure diagnosed case of laziness. Farley, NY turned out to be one of the ugliest, dirtiest, most fowl stops we have seen in a while. In fact, Farley's citizens turned out to be some of the ugliest, dirtiest, and the most fowl people we had encountered too. Really, it was like they have no respect for themselves for the place they called home. A trashcan could be an arm's-length away and they would just drop their garbage right at their feet. Trash everywhere. In three days since we had arrived, there was enough food waste left behind to feed a herd of wild raccoons. And it did. Every night, an army of glowing eyes crept out of the woods, trolling for a feast. And Lord help you if you got in their way!

I couldn't really blame Tully for his sudden bout of ....

whatever it was.

Photo Writing #1

It was meant to be a display of modern art – like "Trash Takes Over the Metropolis." I had grand visions of my giant toilet paper rolls spilling out of a gas – guzzling taxi splashed across the cover of the New York Times, with the caption "Local Artist Makes Profound Statement and Inspires a Movement toward environmental Change." I, or rather my art, would become the poster child for environmental ratification in the country's biggest cities! That was the idea anyway.

Unfortunately, my vision was less than prophetic. In fact, it ended in a overnight jail sentence and a $2000 fine. "You were blocking a fire lane, "they said. "Caused accidents from distracted motorists ", they claimed!

What was wrong with these people, had they no appreciation for modern art? Did they not understand the greater use for these taxis? I was making a statement! A movement for the sake of our planet!

■■

Photo writing #1 (Meteor flying in space)

The alarm rang out sometime near 2 AM. The warning to evacuate immediately. But no one listened, of course. If we got out of bed every time that ear piercing siren went off, dropped everything every time the evacuation chime rang, our lives would be consumed by pointless interruptions. We would spend hours running from or hiding from, imaginary dangers. False warnings issued by paranoid government affiliate.

But this alarm, we would soon learn, was no fake. We were actually in very real, very immediate danger.

We had heard that impact was possible. There was a giant meteor heading directly for earth. There was a chance that the gravitational pull would knock it out of its path. That seemed a lot more likely than the chances of the direct impact. I mean, don't they have space layers or something to annihilate those things? Blow them to specs of dust before they get too close? The science teacher at school had spent the last week warning us of a possible danger of impact. But it really sounded more like a sci-fi novel then reality. We ignored her just like we ignored the alarms. And now here we were, trapped.

<u>704 Superheroes</u> (This is meant to be a short children picture book – pictures incomplete)

We were sprinting across the lot behind the school. The alarm in the room 704 had rung, signaling the need for the 704 Superheroes! A massive catastrophe was threatening to overtake the village of Clifton Park, and everyone in it!

The kids pulled out their secret pouches, stored secretly beneath their desks and placed their body doubles in their seats, before rocketing out of the emergency rescue window. Alex the Amazing was holding his magic poison applesauce ready to drench anything in his path.

Z-force Mike held his Zanny Zipper of doom, awaiting the time to unleash his fury. Madeline the Wise knew exactly how to outsmart any evil-doer and would keep the group in line. Dainty Deirdre possessed the power of charm, and could sweet-talk anyone into submission. Lily had lots of lilies-fierce lucky lilies. If the team ran out of power, all they needed was to wish on one.

Dominating Dom could assemble any tool, weapon, or piece of equipment in seconds and was always ready to help. Harley rode his Harley ahead of the group, checking for danger and reporting back to Grace, the mind reader extraordinaire. Balanced Bruce could stay steady as a cat walks tightropes and climbs trees, bouncing between branches. He kept a lookout from above, guided by Eagle-eye Ethan who watched from the sky. Michael Kanga-Roos and Kitty Katelyn could leap 50 ft. in the air, over buildings, across rivers, they helped the team get where they needed to go. And if they couldn't cross any obstacle, Terri the Twister would knock trees out of the way and Tsunami Salina who would clear the ground below. Saxon could morph into the shape of any dinosaur and provided the greatest scare tactic the team had.

Tatiana the Terrific had the memory of a thousand years- she could read anything and remember it forever.

Husna was another source of great strength, draped in mystery, she could perform great acts of will, resisting any invasion.

When it came to negotiations, Peter the Powerful and Casey the Creative were the team's key players-they could communicate to anyone, in any language.

Meticulous Madison and Menacing Morgan had the power of bending and flipping in any direction- they could fit into places no one else could.

Adrianna was essential as she could sneak around anyone or anything. Light on her feet, she was nearly impossible to detect. While the Jester J's were responsible for distracting the enemy, Joey would yell, Justin would shriek, and Jimmy would scurry around. With them around, no criminal could focus.

And the pack was kept in line by Checkered Chase and Gavin the Great- They ensured no one got too out of line.

However, today was a special case. Their very own town was under attack. As they approached the main road, they knew immediately where the enemy was. Harley took off ahead-assessing the situation. Grace heard his thoughts and reported back to Madeline the Wise. She determined the best method of attack. Saxon became a pterodactyl and joined Eagle-eye Ethan in the sky. Alex the Amazing took the right side, ready to shoot poison sauce, and Mike Z took the left with his zipper of doom.

As they approached the Green-eyed monster, the battle began. Michael Kanga-Roos and Kitty Katelyn sprang into the air, landing on his head and poking his eyes while Meticulous Madison and Menacing Morgan slid between his giant's toes, tickling him until he could stand no more. As he landed, The Jester J's began bouncing and screeching around his head and Husna-The Mysterious was able to tie him down. Always trying to avoid violence, Peter the Powerful and Casey the Creative got to work offering the monster freedom in exchange for his surrender. The monster refused until Dainty Dierdre was able to sweet talk him into submission. Dominating Dom assembled a cage from spare tools and Chase and Gavin led him in. They would release the monster into the river to head back to wherever he came from. The 704 Superheroes were sure he would never comeback. And if he did, Tatiana would remember. Returning to school Adrianna entered first, checking the room and ensuring it was safe. Then one by one, each hero took his or her seat. Carefully returning the body doubles to their secret spots and waited for the bell to ring. Miss Ladu smiled- she had the best class EVER! ....

■■■

2010

"Time has fallen asleep in the afternoon sunshine" –
Ray Bradbury

The little girl loved the sunshine. She loved the sunshine so much that when there was a cloudy day, she felt her entire being settle into a terribly melancholy state. She no longer wanted to rise to meet the day, no longer cared to attend school, surrounded by classmates, laughing and joking. She instead preferred to crawl deep to the end of her bed, beneath the tucked sheet and hide. On cold, rainy fall days like these, she felt more like the wicked witch of the west, trapped inside by the crippling fear of water. As if that one lonely raindrop would send her into a deeper state of depression, one in which she might never recover.

But today was not that day at all. Lilly opened her eyes to the intense strokes of sunlight filtering through her satin curtains, staining the walls in rose colored hues. The one beam of light directed westward to her face, warmed the tip of her nose and caused her to erupt into a sneeze. The day was new and young and Lilly was elated.

She leapt from her bed, landing gracefully on the shag rug like a gazelle escaping the confines of the forest, finding the new, fresh, cool air of the field. Pulling on the linen shorts which lay crumpled by the door and readjusting her lacy white dress, Lilly bound down the stairs, beyond her books, forgetting her breakfast and traversed the drive towards the field of yellow and blue flowers swaying with the breeze … this is what she called heaven.

I stepped out of my third floor condo, trailing the warmth of my white down blanket behind me. Missing the comfortable closeness of my chocolate sheets, my breath was stolen as the damp breeze rustled my loose cotton tee-shirt. I immediately regretted this so-called outdoor carpet taking up residence on my balcony as it held more water than the wood. Now with icy rain water creeping though the bottom of my socks, slogging the spaces in my toes, I wanted so badly to return to the cocoon of my bed, rolled up tight, sealing out the brisk darkness of an Autumn dawn.

A dangling creaking branch scraping the front window panel with a loud screech stole my calm reluctance and startled me alert and back to reality. Peeling off the wet soggy socks, I retreated to the warm confines of the house, past the fresh golden apples and plucked a fun size snickers from the pumpkin jar stash of trick-or-treat candy. Some years back I had convinced myself that the dairy of the chocolate and protein packed peanuts was more than enough to sustain my hunger. A perfect pick me up. Better than leftover pie or toasted pumpkin seeds. Full of nutrients. Of course. So delectable.

■■

Limerick

I wanted to feed my cat
She was sitting on a mat
But from a shoe
She ate some glue
And then forever she sat

I had a tall glass for Jim
But didn't think to inform him
And couldn't deny
The poison inside
Had just been used to kill him

I borrowed my mother's new car
Didn't tend to drive too far
But I crashed into a tree
Cuz I couldn't quite see
When I stumbled out of the bar

■■

She stands silently at the peak of the stairs. Wrapped in the still coolness radiated by the pale banana laminate jacket. Breathing silently, shallowly, as to avoid revealing her presence to any wondering passerby. Removing her coat, she crumples her shirt cuffs into damp balls, twisted to roses by her finger tips, absorbing droplets of moisture meant to cool her nerves. She wonders if her shrunken, puffy eyelids depreciate the anticipation and elation which pulse through her veins. She hopes her pale blue eyes still hold the same warm comfort for him that they always did. A tear or two have been shed in recent hours, made all the worse by a dedicated focus to the road. A six-hour journey to arrive where her feet now stand, sheltered in chocolate fuzz boots. The only sense of comfort for her now. She shifts from one foot to the other now, wondering how she looked most appealing. How she could still hold the same magnetic desire she possessed before the war.

Fractured Fairy Tale (10/13/10)

Jack and Jill were married under very interesting circumstances. Jack was the son of a very peculiar individual known for climbing castle walls, only to fall from them, crack his skull, and simply repeat the same ridiculous action once he was cured. Unfortunately, one fall was from a rather high wall and despite the best actions of all the king's horses and all the king's men, he just could not be put back together again.

Jack inevitably inherited some of his father's clumsiness. This was not to terrible at first, not until his father was gone did Jack begin to feel very alone. Jill, on the other hand, was a very empathetic person. She understood what being alone felt like. Jill was born with a terrible malady which caused her nose to grow every time she lied. This not only made her relatively unattractive, but inspired a candidness which many found offensive. She spent much time alone that was, until she met Jack. They were married in late spring at the precise moment the cat jumped over the moon. Serenaded by a song above the star twinkling, the two exchanged vows in their back yard, shaded by the hill to the west.

■■■

Quotes

"Be careful what you wish for, you just might get it all"
    – Chris Daughtry

"I just gotta get myself over me' – The Format

"Don't cry because it's over, smile because it happened"
    – Dr. Seuss

"I meant what I said what I meant" – Dr. Seuss

"It's better to be absolutely ridiculous than absolutely boring" – Marilyn Monroe

"The best thing about the future is that it only comes one day at a time" – Abraham Lincoln

Free Verse Poem (11/1/10)

I giggled when the cat tumbled from the tree
I poked it with a stick
I sobbed when the sun came out
And chased off the clouds
I rolled my eyes when the vows were said
Knew they would never last
Absolutely ridiculous but never ever boring

I cracked a smile at the funeral
No one liked him anyway
I stuck my tongue out at the widow
She seemed to need a laugh
I managed to cry at Disney
It was just too damn happy
Absolutely ridiculous but never ever boring

I teased the child with candy but
Never handed it over
I stole the old man's walker
It made for a good prop
Slashed the priests' tires
Just because I could
Absolutely ridiculous, never ever boring

*****

Santa Santa please tell me
When again will I see Mommy
Grandma said she went away
But couldn't tell me how long she'd stay
Before she left, we hugged goodbye
She looked back at me with a heavy sigh
But now my 8th birthday is past
And Thanksgiving is coming fast.
Then it will be Christmas day
And all I really want is to say
I love you mom and miss you tons
Come home to, your only son
Pick me up and hold me tight
Tell me stories into the night
And tuck me in where I will lay
And promise me this time you'll stay.

■■

I awoke to a new life

With new stories

And new days

To a peaceful place where I could live

And I could grow

You only held me back

You only held me down

I found love with someone new

With bright days, ahead that you will never know

I don't need you anymore

You can stay where you are, same routine same old days

Stuck in this town, your same old ways

Like a broken record, your story plays

But I really hope

When he leaves me, hurts me

I can come back to you

I can cry to you

Won't you be there for me

Won't you dry my tears

I didn't do anything wrong.

Winter Sonnet

Winter is the very best time of year
Giving all the children lots of candy
I love the sound of all the Christmas cheer

The happy faces make me feel dandy
When we pick out our fresh cut Christmas tree
I can't wait to get home and hang the lights
To fill my home with happiness and glee

Gazing out the window at the festive sights
I stand beneath the hanging mistle-toe
And wait for my special holiday kiss
Surrounded by the winter whiteness glow

This is the time that I would never miss
The hugs and smiles and cards that I send
Can't wait for winter time to come again

Appeloosa was a very red, round sweet thing. She spent her days basking in the sun rays as they stream in between the blinds, moving gradually East to West. She finds that the sun is nearly unbearable by noon but fades away with the rotation of the earth. Yet she sits unmoved, enjoying the heat. When the sun washes of red and yellow caress the horizon, her panic begins. She can almost hear the patter of little feet beating on the steps, climbing to the front door as the school bus pulls away. She dreads the children's return, knowing they will demand attention creating noise and searching for a snack. Oh, the dreaded snack – the children could never decide. They would rummage through the cabinets, refrigerator – choosing one thing then discarding for another.

remember to smile.

■■■ ■■■

The True 3-Little Pigs

I bought this wonderful little house in a quiet part of the woods where I knew, no, I thought that no pesky little rodents would be able to drive me crazy with all their craziness and squealing.

Well wouldn't you know, I hadn't been there a week before I started hearing those little pig's pitter pattering outside of my house. At first it wasn't so bad, they just passed by on their way to the market but then it turned into passing thru on the way to work, on the way to visit Hansel and Gretel, everywhere they went it seemed they had to come thru my yard. I thought I had my anger under control but then I realize every time they passed by, they were steeling parts of my house straw from the roof, wood from the siding, and bricks from chimney.

I couldn't take it anymore. So, I put on my Sunday best and headed to their houses to retrieve what was mine and request that they please not return to torment me or destroy my house any further. Much to my surprise, I was greeted with a rather displeased squealing and carrying on while the pigs launched food and spices at my head.

Then, of all things, a pepper shaker! Well let it be known that pepper makes me, like many others, sneeze uncontrollably. It just crept up on me and before I knew it, I had blown that straw house with one sold sneeze. Any my second sneeze, as I always sneeze in two's, blew the stick house right out of town. (The rest is history)

*****

The Roadrunner and Wylie Coyote have historically been at odds, but in a playful way. Blowing one another up, tripping the other over a cliff, or dropping on the other a very heavy object was simply part of their enduring friendship.

What better way to bond with one of my fellow day-care buddies than to follow the Coyote's lead. As I placed the small silver tack pointed up upon my buddie's seat, I anxiously awaited. I hoped her trip to the pencil sharpener wasn't too long as a teacher might pass by and discover my bonding attempt.

Alas! The grinding noise of a pencil and lead stopped and I knew she was returning. I sat quietly in my seat, glancing over to be sure the small silver point was still in place. My buddy traversed the room while admiring her artistic sculpture of a pencil point and plopped firmly down in her seat. I would not have appeared so guilty had her tonsil rattling scream and subsequent topple off the chair caused me to stare in utter astonishment and then laugh. We were real friends now. A regular old Roadrunner and Coyote. Too bad no one understood.

▪▪

The Leprechaun

Eric the Leprechaun lived high atop Mont Oval overlooking the quaint village below. Although the village folk only saw Eric once in a while and only for seconds at a time, they knew all about him. They knew Eric had a large sum of money in the form of gold. They knew that he kept his gold in a large pot which he proudly displayed on the peak of Mount Oval. They knew that Eric would never share this month with anyone, Eric was a greedy leprechaun.

One day, King Paul of Mount Oval Village learned of a terrible storm coming their way. It was said that the storm was causing giant waves to crash in from the sea, creating raindrops the size of cows! King Paul was very upset. He knew that his village folk had very weak roofs and very thin doors. This storm was sure to wash out the entire village. "If only we could buy new doors and roofs, we might outlast the storm" he thought, but where would he get that kind of money from? King Paul looked up the mountain and saw the pot of gold. Since the people of Mount Oval Village were such honest people, he knew they couldn't steal it. But surely Eric the Leprechaun would understand and be willing to help.

King Paul began the journey up the mountain, through the thick trail of shamrocks. When he found Eric the Leprechaun, he was sitting on his gold pile juggling coins and humming to himself. King Paul knew that he would not be able to blink for many minutes now for everyone knows you cannot look away from a leprechaun or he will surely disappear. "Eric the Leprechaun" King Paul pleaded. "We are in a desperate situation. The storm is coming quick but we cannot afford to prepare for it. Could you so kind as to lend us some of your gold? Surely we could repay you."

"He he he he" Eric squealed, "you want my gold? He he he he, I don't need to give you anything until you follow that rainbow to the end." He pointed to the sky. "What rainbow Eric?" the King asked as he looked to the sky. Eric didn't answer. He was gone.

King Paul knew he couldn't win with a greedy leprechaun so he began back down the mountain. He was sad and very, very nervous.

The next day, the sky turned dark stately black. The clouds swirled and crashed into one another. The village folk huddled in fear as a loud roar came closer and closer. A wave for sure!

Bosh! cling cling cling cling … Silence. The village people opened their shutters and peeked outside, sure there was damage of some sort.

What they found was not damage but rather gold showered across the village and rainbows beaming in all directions. And Eric the leprechaun washed to the to the base of the mountain in his empty pot.

■■

There was once a beautiful Princess who lived in her father's castle. She was a very spoiled little girl. She spent all her days wandering around the castle and telling her two evil stepsisters what to do. They had to listen to her because, after all, she was royalty. The Princess was always complaining too. Nothing she had was good enough, she always wanted better.

One night when she laid in her bed, she decided that it was too uncomfortable for her. She stomped down the hall and threw open her father's chamber door.

"Father!!" she cried. He arose startled.

"What is it now?" he replied.

"It's my bed, it is just not suitable for a Princess!" she said.

Her father, fed up with all this complaining by his spoiled daughter, decided to teach her a lesson. He told her that she needed to learn a lesson and to go sleep on the palace wall. Then she would appreciate the nice soft bed that she has inside. The Princess was very upset at this order but did what she was told. After all, she really wanted the pink Lamborghini for her birthday next week.

While she was sleeping, the Princess had an awful nightmare … she began tossing and turning causing her to fall off the wall. All of the kings' horses and all the king's men heard her call for help but decided to ignore her because she was probably just playing a joke on them, which she often did. She liked to see them coming to her rescue and then laughing.

But this time she really needed help and no one came. The Princess realized she had fallen into the woods outside the palace walls, a place she had never been before. She spent the whole night looking for the entrance back into the palace but only got more and more lost. Around dawn, she saw a little girl in a red and white checked cape carrying a basket. The Princess decided to follow the girl, hoping she would lead her back to town. Instead, they came upon a house. On the door, it read "Grandma's House". The Princess hid behind a tree for a moment then decided to knock on the door. After all, she was the Princess, they had to let her in. She knocked and then entered. There were no lights besides the one near the bed. She went to the bed where there was a horribly ugly grandmother.

"Oh, what big eyes you have" the Princess said. "The better to see you with." Replied grandmother.

"Oh, and your ears, they are giant and furry!", "The better to hear you with!"

"And your teeth! They are giant and sharp!" "The better to eat you with" the grandmother said as she pulled off her cap and revealed herself as a wolf. The wolf plunged at the Princess and tried to bite her. Instead, he bit her crown and it got stuck in his teeth. The Princess dashed through the door and kept running and running. Soon she was too tired to run anymore and decided to look for a place to rest. She laid beside a tree and feel fast asleep.

When she awoke, the Princess was being carried by seven dwarfs wearing pointy hats. They were discussing amongst themselves where to bring her, they decided that the three little houses built by the friendly pigs was the closest. Which of the three little pig's houses should they lay her in, the house made of straw, the house made of twigs or the house made of bricks. One of the dwarfs chirped in and informed his worker friends that the one made of straw and twigs had both been destroyed by all the huffing and puffing of the evil wolf. This terrified the Princess, she had just escaped the wolf as did these poor little pigs in their houses. She decided to lay still in order to avoid startling the dwarfs. After they had laid the Princess in bed, the dwarfs sat around to rest. The Princess tossed and turned in the hard, bumpy bed. Finally, she couldn't take it anymore.

■■■

Dog in Subway Photo (10/18/13)

This is Bob. Bob is a sad dog. Because today was not Bob's day. It began yesterday when Bob's friend, the Tall Man who feeds him, was getting ready for work. Instead of just packing a sandwich and apple, the man also packed a banana, granola bar, and an extra soda. Bob had a feeling this wasn't a good sign. He knew from experience that when the Tall Man packed this much food, it could only mean one thing – he was working late. And that meant Bob would have to wait a very, very long time for his dinner and nightly walk. And he was right. The Tall Man took so long to come home, Bob's tummy was growling!

So today, when Bob saw the man packed extra food, he decided he would go along to work with Tall man. Of course, Tall Man was not aware of this plan and did not notice when Bob slipped out the apartment door behind him.

All the way down the block, through the crowded sidewalks and past busy coffee shops, Bob followed Tall Man. He stayed right on his heels, down the steps and into the subway station.

But then Bob stopped. He watched as Tall Man, along with hundreds of others crowded into a train, with little room left. Bob realized then that he would not fit. He couldn't get on that train and he couldn't follow Tall Man to work.

Slouching down to the cold, dirty tiled floor, Bob suddenly became very sad. Not only was he going to be alone all day, but he couldn't even go home. He came all this way and he had no idea from where. And Tall Man had no idea Bob was out. Would this be it? Would Bob be left here forever?

*****

People on the Cliff   10/18/13

The Jepsen family had had a rough year. It seemed that every month was filled with some traumatic event or tragedy.

It started in January with little Jenny. Jenny was an amazing gymnast. She trained for 6 hours every

Saturday, not to mention hour-long private lessons during the week. She was destined to be the next Olympic gymnast. That was until she attempted that back handspring on the beam. Flipping backward, she had missed the beam by inches, landing sideways on the floor, and shattering her left arm. Jenny proceeded to spend the next several weeks in a cast before being told she would need surgery.

February went on, rather uneventfully, which meant March was going to be rough. And it was. While driving to Jenny's doctor, the Jepsen's car slid on some ice and ran sideways into a stop sign. Everyone was okay, but the car was not. Now the family was left with one car to use. This wouldn't have been so bad except for Jenny's doctor's appointments, Alex's soccer and baseball practice, and Mom and Dad working very far apart. It had become nothing short of a juggling act to get everyone where they needed to be.

This juggling act made everyone so stressed out, no one even smiled anymore. So, when it came time for a Christmas card picture, Mom knew exactly what to do. If her family wouldn't smile, she would hire a stand-in family, one who would smile. After searching high and low, she found 2 kids and 2 adults, who looked similar enough to pass for them and away they went – a fake family for a photoshoot.

It sounded like a brilliant plan, until the Christmas cards went out. Mom was not prepared for the backlash she got. No one understood and everyone was upset.

*****

The dancers danced their dance and the waltzers waltzed their waltz. The servers passed their plates and the girls garbled their gossip. But behind the mirage of decadent gowns lurked a malicious scheme. Tonight was not just a night of festive celebration. Tonight, they would learn, would be a night of panic and horror and mischievous motives.

Mya's head rested on her pink satin pillowcase, her eyes wide open, her mind on only one thing. She had just celebrated her 13th birthday which meant that she was not allowed to attend the holiday Gala. The kids were usually taken to the local theater to see the newest animation, while the adults donned themselves in silk ties and billowing gowns. Year after year, Mya watched her mother delicately pinning her hair in tiny loose curls and lining her lips with a shimmery red lipstick. The lipstick reminded Mya of the glass Christmas ornaments on the family tree and more than anything, she wanted to see the hall of trees at the Gala. And this year she would.

Pulling back the bed's canopy, she slid her feet into the slippers she got for her birthday. Because after all, she was an adult now, and adults wear slippers.

Reed hated his parents. Well, he hated them today. In fact, he had hated them for the last two years, around this time of year. His friends had all been allowed to attend the holiday gala alone. Why did his parents insist on him escorting a girl? Why did he even have to go at all? In silent protest, he sat at the breakfast table, cheerios untouched, absorbing milk. He wished he was a Cheerio, cheerios didn't have to go to Gala's.

In a great big closet, in a great big bedroom, in a great big house, Sara stood before the gowns. It was the second year she would be allowed to attend the holiday Gala. But it would be the first year she would actually go. She stared absently at the frilly lavender crinoline, leaning against the mirror-like sheer of the yellow satin. She had two choices, and it wasn't in dresses. Choosing between last year's trendy Chanel or this year's Gucci couture was easy, this decision would be so much larger.

Lea understood the expectation. She understood what she was supposed to do, how she was supposed to act, the people she was supposed to be with. After all, she had been raised in high society, with money, and all the problems that often accompanied it. So she also understood why she was Reed Biltmore's escort to the Holiday Gala. The Biltmore name carried with it connotations of power and control. The family was of old money- having inherited a sum which could make the queen blush. Reed spent his summers in Europe, on the family's vineyard. He was polished and refined. Years of boarding school had left him with the mannerisms of a prince. For a girl, her introduction as an adult could not be any more meaningful and significant than doing so on Reed Biltmore's arm. She would begin her journey through high society a few steps above the other girls. She may even be invited to join the exclusive ranks of the Carroway Society. A girl in her position would literally have the world handed to her on a gold platter, rather than the silver one she already had. But silver and gold were too heavy- she preferred something lighter. She thought back to a chemistry lesson. She remembers how much lighter aluminum was than most other metals – all the while looking like silver, and costing much less. One thing, outwardly appearing as something else. How appropriate, she thought.

Mya skipped down the marble staircase and through the grand foyer. Her slippers made a soft patter on the stone and she couldn't wait to hear the echo of her heels as she graced down the stairs later. Plopping down beside her brother, she couldn't help but to notice how miserable he looked.

"Perk up Buttercup! It's Galla day!"

Reed looked up from his Cheerios whirlpool, "and what are you so chipper about?"

"Well it is only the single greatest day of my entire life! Think about it-the sparkling trees with their twinkling lights lining the grand entranceway where I will grace all with my presence. And they will all look at me with my grand gown and shimmering lips and wonder who this spectacular demonstration of opulence might be!"

"Stop, you are going to make me vomit into your breakfast."

"Oh don't worry, I'm not going anywhere near carbohydrates today – they might bloat my face and I need to look perfect!"

"I don't think anything could make your head any bigger than it already is "Reed grumbled under his breath.

"What are you so miserable about anyway, at least you get to come home from St. Anthony's for the weekend. And besides, you get to escort one of the most beautiful girls available".

*****

Rhyming Poem

I like pink
And I like blue
But I don't like mink
Inside my shoe

Purple's alright
And so is green
Red starts a fight
Because he is so mean

When I'm sad I like yellow
Or maybe some black
It makes me feel mellow
Instead of attack

Orange is one
That I like the most
Color of sun
Or rotting toast

Who could like brown
It just isn't mine
Looks so dirty
Makes me frown

"Bill made me a Criminal"

I love to swim. I grew up swimming. I grew up spending my summers at camp, on the lake. For me, water is just part of my life. So when I meet someone who can't swim, it seems strange to me. I mean, doesn't everyone know how to swim? I used to think so, and that was my first mistake.

I never really brought my friends to my camp before. It is kind of far away and there are so many other things to do in the summer. But this particular weekend was quiet. So, I gathered up a few friends, some burgers for the grill and headed to Galway Lake.

It was a gorgeous day. The sun was shining, a light breeze was blowing and the lake was calm. It was perfectly peaceful- almost too peaceful! Boring perhaps. But what could we do? Kayaking seemed like a good option. We put the boys to work gathering the supplies. We borrowed a few kayaks from the neighbors but left the life jackets behind. It seemed unnecessary on a calm day on a private lake with no waves.

It was clear from the way Vohan and Bill were carrying the kayaks that they were not exactly outdoorsy people and they were definitely not kayakers. And when they tried to climb into the kayaks one foot at a time- repeatedly slipping in the boat – I should have known this would be an interesting trip around the lake. They looked a little like two zebras in swimsuits trying to climb into a mini-cooper. Ridiculous.

When we finally pushed off the shore and began the journey across the calm water, it was surprisingly easy. We laughed and talked. Sunbathed and smiled. And then we had to turn around.

I demonstrated for the others how to push forward with one side of the oar and backwards with the other side. I easily spun around. I could see out of the corner of my eye, at least a couple of the others were close behind. But that was the problem. There were only two other people behind me, not the three I had set out with. Where was Bill? The water was so calm, the boats traveled swiftly and we had gone quite a way from where we turned. The three of us looked at each other - partly in confusion, and partly in disbelieve that we have possibly lost our friend – I mean, that only happens in horror stories- right? Was Bill at the bottom of the lake? Gone forever? Part of me wondered if I would go to jail for this. He had a lifejacket, after all, or did we leave them behind. He was a grown adult who could swim, right? And then it occurred to me. I never asked Bill if he could swim. And I never did offer him a lifejacket. Bill was dead. And I was a criminal.

But then I saw it. The Zebra in a mini-cooper. But now the mini-cooper, or rather the kayak was upside down, and Bill the Zebra was trying desperately to climb on top. That's when I realized – Bill couldn't swim and if I didn't do something- this wasn't going to end well. Even though I was fully dressed in normal clothes, I immediately dove in. I pulled at the water and kicked furiously. I fought with all of my might and reached Bill in record time for me. He was so tired from trying to climb on top of the boat and almost completely out of breath. I'm not sure he was thinking clearly as he immediately clung to my back, pulling me under too. Now I was gasping and gagging as the water was filling my nose. I had no other choice. I pried Bill's fingers off my shirt and swam away from him, taking his kayak with me. It was the only solution. Otherwise we were both going to drown.

When we had a few feet between us, I was able to flip his kayak enough for him to have a place to grab on to. I pulled it back to him, handed him the seat cushion and hooked a rope from the boat to his belt. And then I swam – boat and boy in tow.

I was able to pull us back to shallow water and Bill was okay. But I learned that day – never assume anything.

Melinda made her way down the snow lined street, her every step mirrored in the deep cold wetness. She had purchased these overpriced snow boats assuming they would keep her feet warm and dry in the snow...or at least that's how she justified spending $200 that she really didn't have. But as she rounded 89th Street, the frigid wetness began to make its way through the Australian boots and seep between her toes, every step becoming more unbearable. It reminded her of picking out Christmas trees with her father. After her parents split up, her father decided to become some kind of "Super Dad". And his idea of the perfect Christmas tree, or Super-tree, could only be found on the coldest, wettest, darkest day. In the furthest, deepest, ugliest part of the woods. He saw it as bonding time, Melinda thought more of torture time. Minutes in that freezing air felt like hours, yards felt like miles, and the magic of the tree was somehow lost in the misery.

Melinda thought she had left all that behind her when she came to the city. But her damp socks told her otherwise. Her toes ached and her heart was cold. The "magic" of the season was lost on her. There were too many tourists clogging traffic on the sidewalks. Too many black-market peddlers wielding knock off handbags in the way. Most of her friends had gone home to their suburban roots, and left her to occupy herself with Netflix and take-out. And that was perfectly fine with her. In fact, she was looking forward to the peace and quiet. She had every intention of burying herself in a sea of blankets and no intention of facing the chill outside, or the people outside, or the snow, she was definitely over the snow.

As she cased the final......

*****

She couldn't help it, she gasped for air as her face twisted into knots, hair glued down by tears and eyes as red as the heart that was being torn out of her chest. Just come back breathing. Just come back alive.

No, we aren't going to the same place we did the first time. That was a special mission, this time we're going to be out in the dessert, I'm talking straight up sand as far as you can see. I won't be able to call you. But just keep writing to me, I want to know what you're doing every day. Send me pictures. Lots of them.

Sweetheart, I don't want you down here when I leave.

She wanted to watch the bus turn out of the parking lot and stand amongst all of the other proud wives and mothers as their prized possessions, soldiers, began the long, listless journey to their home for the next 6, 7, 8, months. The women would stand around the hot North Carolina sun in sweet dresses, weeping for their heroes, waving flags of encouragement and blowing kisses that would be lost in the cloud of dust and sand. She wanted to cry with them, bond with them, feel the fear of watching a loved leave. But he said no…it was better that way. Get a ride to the base, find a place to stay, find a ride back to the airport… with no help, silly idea. Besides, those women lived with their beloved. They had only been dating 5 months. And long distance at that.

I have to go now, I need to throw away my cell phone. I love you so much, stop crying, you'll be okay. Sweetheart, I love you.

Class was in a half an hour. How was she supposed to sit through her 28-year-old Mexican professor drone on about how on mitochondria replicate with swollen eyes and only one thing on her mind? It didn't matter, she was failing anyway.

"Hey you!" Jeremy didn't turn off his phone yet so he let me use it but he's getting disconnected in 20 minutes. "How ya doing? Ya'right? It's only 6 months sweetheart. I'll be fine. Okay I gotta go now. I love you. Write to me!"

The cell phone. Slowly becoming a permanent fixture to human bodies, much like glasses or acrylic nails. It goes with us to the bathroom, to the dinner table, to work and to bed. It follows our every motion, our every action, our every chore. Her fixture was worse. The small silver flip phone remained attached to her hand by a skinny silver strap slipped loosely over her wrist. The phone, the best friend. Because perhaps, just maybe, that phone would ring for her. Perhaps it would be the bearer of the most horrific news she could imagine. Perhaps it would be his mother on the other line asking her to come over immediately. Perhaps not. Perhaps it would be a call saying he was on his way back to her because the loneliness drove him to insanity, and the docs sent him back. If she only knew. The phone, her best friend.

Her phone rang. "Hey!"

Her heart dropped, stomach twisted, eyes welled up again. She stopped dead in her tracks, fell onto her squeaky dorm bed and laid in the exact spot she knew she was sure to get service on her cell phone. She motioned for her roommate to shut the door and stared out the window. She smiled as she listened to his voice, asked him about the trip, asked why it took 15 days to get there, asked everything one could ask in 5 minutes. "We are at the air force base in Bagram, I can't really talk but I wanted to call you, I probably won't be able to again, at least not for a very long time. I love you sweetheart. How ya doing? Alright? Did you write to me yet? I love you, buh bye."

Did the call help? Did it make it harder? He called her. He could have called his mom, but he called her. She knew that. She loved him. The phone, her best friend.

Babe, Hi! You called me today, you made me so incredibly happy! ....

One day they just stopped. The letters, they must have been lost. The must have had a longer delay than usual. Two weeks was bad, but maybe it was getting worse. Maybe with the holidays coming the mail got slower. No, the holidays were months away. Maybe he was busy. Maybe he was out in the field too much. Maybe they were just lost. He still called when he could. But the letters.... they were more romantic...

Maybe the phones were down. Maybe a wind storm took them out. Maybe he was in the field again. She knew she was lucky for the calls she did get. She knew she was lucky for the last 6 months. They were not near phones. He'll be home any day. He's just busy.

No, the phones aren't down and he isn't busy. What's the problem? Are you sick of me? Of my cute packages? Are you sick of having to call me every time you are near a phone? Are you in love with some chick writing dear john letters? She hated him. Two weeks, no call.

Now this is really bad, your mother talked to you yesterday, you didn't call me. That's terrific. And she said you had an infection, terrific, so you are on bed rest and you still can't call me? You never call your mom. I'm more important. Or so I thought. Terrific. You're welcome. You're welcome for everything that I have done for you, for waiting 6 months for you, for driving your mother around and pretending to like her. You're welcome for the canned food and rocker magazines. You're welcome for the endless devotion and for the times I missed while waiting here for you. She really hated him.

Birthday weekend. All alone. No call. No letter.

She went to a place she knew she shouldn't be. She followed her adventurous nature down a lengthy paved interstate. She found herself in front of another dorm. One full of young men. She found herself at a friend's dorm, drinking cheap beer and blowing cigarette smoke from his fourth-floor window. Still no call. She found herself wandering the streets with locals and friends. She found herself sober and cursing about the time she wasted waiting for a false hope. She found herself feeling stupid for the effort she had made without the slightest reciprocation. She found herself sad.

But she was so wrong and the truth soon came to light.

He found himself so sick out in the heat of the desert. Not wanting to look like the guy who couldn't "take it", he forged on. Days turned into weeks and it was getting worse. He remembers looking up into the sky and looking at the sun, the same sun his honey would be looking at half way around the world. Things got dark.

The next thing he remembers is opening his eyes and looking up at a florescent light hanging over his bed. Bed? When did he get a bed? The nurse noticed he was awake and called for a Doctor. When the Dr. approached his bedside he asked a lot of personal questions, what is your name, rank, parents alive, contact information ... it seemed endless. I was exhausted and had a lot of questions myself.

They took my vitals and documented the information in a gray metal flip chart that was attached to the end of my bed. It smelled military. Then they proceeded to explain that I had Leukemia and they could not treat me there in Germany. I would be sent back to the states for treatment and I needed to contact my parents.

I remember the call with my mother, her religious beliefs are so strong and allowed us to be thankful for the time we have had and to leave it to God, he will take care of everything. Doctors are no longer necessary. After we spoke I tried to call my honey – but the phone just rang with no answer. I guess I'll just have to try again when I get home.

A couple days pass and I find myself back in the states for treatment. Unfortunately, my cancer is not curable but there is not a lot of information available on how to treat someone with this condition. I have to do something – I'm deteriorating quickly.

She finally gets a call from her Babe and can't believe what she's hearing – she was so wrong and is kicking herself for thinking the way she did … of course he loved her, he needs her! She would be by his side for however long it takes and will do everything in her powers to find a treatment or cure. This can't be happening, they are so young and have so much ahead of them! Without even a thought, she leaves her class, runs back to the apartment, grabs a small bag and throws as many things she can gather in 5 minutes or less. She calls her mom and lets her know that she's leaving town and will call her when she arrives, not to worry.

She stayed by his side every day from then on and was with him right up to his last minute. They talked for hours and hours, days turned into nights and it was difficult to know which was which from their small hospital room in the corner of the wing. Days turned to weeks, weeks to months, but months never turn to years.

When he left, he took a part of her with him ... she never finds the same love again ... until she joins him.

*****

Dear Mom,

I was laying here and began to think. I thought how confused you would be when I didn't come home tonight and what you must be thinking as you read this letter. So, I thought I'd clear everything up for you, help you rest easier.

Mom, I remember what you said to me as I walked out the front door. You said, "be a good girl." Of course, I rolled my eyes and waved to you in a rush to leave. I was so happy; you were actually letting me go out with this boy. The boy I had been obsessed with forever (or so it seemed.) I was on cloud nine and I wasn't going to let anything ruin this night. I wasn't going to drink, I promised you I wouldn't, and I wasn't going to do any drugs, I promised Daddy that I wouldn't. And I didn't. So, what happened?

Chris and I pulled out of the driveway and decided that instead of going to dinner like I said I was doing, we would drive around and see what kind of things were happening, on this cool summer night. We drove and we talked and we drove and we talked, it was fun, we had so much in common so much to talk about. I remembered passing a small purple restaurant in the middle of nowhere joking to Chris about it. Soon though, I didn't see purple anymore, I saw a bright flash of light in front of my eyes, like someone had just taken a picture right in my face. Then I saw a blue, dark midnight blue, the same color as Chris' car that we had been in all night. But then, everything was dark and all I could hear were faint voices getting further and further away.

Mom, I started floating and I was so comfortable, like I was on a giant pillow watching everyone beneath me. There were police, and two cars. The cars, one blue and one green were collided. The green car was smashed right into the passenger's side of the blue car. What a shame. It was terrible, there was blood just draining onto the ground and beer bottles everywhere. It was dark out and me, being the curious person that I am, had to know what was going on. So, I approached one of the policemen and asked what happened or if I could help but he ignored me. He must have been really busy. There was a boy, about my age just standing in the middle of the road so I asked him what happened and he ignored me too.

After standing around for a while, I saw you mom, you were crying, did you know the person in the passenger's side seat? Did you know the person driving the green car? Was she a friend of yours? You picked up one of the beer bottles that had fallen out of the green car and collapsed onto the ground. But you too, ignored me. I just wanted to give you a hug. When some of the commotion died down, they pulled a man out of the driver's seat of the green car and covered him with a white sheet, I guess he didn't survive the accident. Then, they pulled a girl out of the passenger's side of the blue car and covered her with a sheet. You turned and threw that beer bottle at the green car and it shattered. Mom, what was wrong? Everyone was leaving so I thought I would too. I thought you might want to be alone so I went to find my own way home.

I was cold now but felt warmth coming from behind me. This heat, it was coming from a light. So. I blew you a kiss and went to the light. And soon, it all made sense. I love you mommy please don't cry. I'll see you soon enough just promise me, you won't drink and drive.

Love always and forever, Your little Angel

9/28/11

     Blasted into a world not all unfamiliar but still relatively new, Erica returned to the lake down south that she had grown to love but was forced to leave. With a car full of novels and stiletto heels, she embarked on a journey, destined to make or break her teaching career. Homeschooling was fun, teaching at her ala mater was exciting. But how would the CMS district treat her. How would she do in a world of southern drawl and cornfields? Would she change or get caught up in her efforts to change the world?

*****

     Lost in the world of delusions and mystery, Tina struggled to maintain her grip on reality through the ebbs and flows every day. She knew she must be a normal girl. She had a normal name, ate normal food. But somehow, she was different. People came to see her daily. They spoke to her in strange tones and threw pans full of lasagna at her. And though the bugs got pretty bad at night, she was forced to sleep outside. Would she ever find out the truth? Was it only a matter of time before someone would tell her? Because Tina didn't know that she was a llama.

*****

When she handed it over, I was thrilled. Never in my life had I been trusted with something so clear, so personal. I never met someone who trusted me this much. But she did and I had no idea why. I pushed it down into my pocket, way down. Past the crease in my leg so as to not risk its mistakenly working its way out. As so many things I do- I rested my hand on it, curling my fingers lightly around the cloth enclosure. Pulling my hand from the skin-hugging denim, I was careful not to slide it from the safety of my hip. I walked around carefully, occasionally tapping the outside of my pocket to ensure the bundle was safely inside. I can't say that I spent much time thinking about anything else that day. I was so enthralled with the trust placed in me, I didn't want to let her down.

The day crawled by in my obsessive paranoia. And when my 3-year-old niece crawled up my leg, pulling my shirt tight, I was relieved. Aunt Mary, can I have my pet rock now please? I signed relief that I was free of this responsibility. Relieved that I had not let this Princess down. Relieved that I deserved the trust placed in me. But as I reached into my pocket, I found something I had not expected. I found a hole. Small enough to miss but large enough to lose a rock. Avery's special rock.

*****

I just want to say one thing to you because I spent most of my night last night freaked out that you were gonna crawl into my bed and try to snuggle with me. I felt like I had to nail my door shut. So that's exactly what I did. I ripped a 2x4 off the ceiling rafters and drove 4 inch stakes through the molding just so that your disgusting face couldn't come over and try something!

But...

No, Stop, this is my time to talk. I've heard enough from you. Always trying to be cool, trying to be the important one. Trying to tell people what to do. Well I got news for you- No one cares. No one even likes or cares about you. You are a washed-up reject.

Well I never!

No, save it. I'm already late for work. As it is, I'm going to have to sneak in the mailroom door so Mr. Toope doesn't see me. I just wanted to get this off my chest and let you know you should lose my number.

Hey!

WHAT!

Umm!

Wait, what? Hello?

Hey. I believe you have the wrong number, this is Mr. Toope.

■■

Story of Lemonade

Memeana was never a happy child. From the day she was born, she crawled around her playpen noticing how her toys' batteries died after only a few plays. Then, they were useless and simply in the way. The world was certainly a sour, bitter place.

When Memeana began to walk, she found that she did not like all the windows which lit up the room and showed all the dirt and dust floating in the air. The world was certainly a sour, bitter place.

When Memeana was finally allowed to play in the yard, she decided she did not like the grass as it itched her ankles when she ran. She did not like the bees that buzzed around her head and tried to sting her. The world was certainly a sour, bitter place.

When Memeana began to help her family work on their lemon farm, she noticed how horrible it was to work with a fruit that no one really liked. She did not like that she was responsible for filling the hummingbird feeder with that thick sugar water which made her fingers stick together. The world was certainly a sour, bitter place.

Now Memeana was about to start school, she hoped to find something good and sweet in the world but once again was sadly disappointed. As she sat through lunch alone, she immediately decided that all the other children were unfriendly and mean as not one of them had attempted to be her friend. But then again, she hadn't tried either. The next day wasn't any better. "Memeana," Miss Spring called out while teaching a poetry lesson, "What is the most beautiful thing you have ever seen?"

Memeana, shocked that anyone was speaking to her, glanced around the room at all of the eager eyes of the curious children. "I have never seen anything beautiful." Everyone in the class giggled and Miss Spring's usually shining smile melted.

"Well that's too bad Memeana. Maybe you are just not noticing the good in the world."

Memeana suck down in her seat and decided that she would never, ever return to school again.

The next morning, Memeana got dressed for school but rather than start the trek to Shining Heights Elementary, she found a spot beneath the lemon trees where she frequently hung the hummingbird feeder. Sinking down against the trunk, she closed her eyes and wished the world wasn't such a sour, bitter place.

Before Memeana had realized she had fallen asleep, she awoke to a splash of a sour, bitter, yet pleasantly sweet mixture on her lips. Memeana sat up with a jolt searching all around for the evil, bitter person responsible for such a joke. What she found was a lemon that had fallen from a tree and landed in a hummingbird feeder above her head, splashing the liquid into her mouth.

Upset at first by the violent wake from her rest, Memeana began to think about this potion made of lemons which she found rather pleasing. Could it be? Could there be something in this world that wasn't so terrible? She plucked a few lemons from the tree and hurried to the kitchen where she immediately mixed up some of the liquid which had startled her.

She dug a pail out of her pile of discarded toys to hold the mixture. The sun streaming through the windows lit the kitchen enough for her to measure just the right amount of sugar.

Eager to share her discovery with the world, Memeana taped a lid on the pail and dashed to school. She burst through the classroom door, interrupting a very serious lesson on bees and their importance for pollination.

"Miss Spring! Miss Spring! I found something beautiful!" Pouring a glass for everyone in the class, Memeana beemed a wide grin.

"MMMMmmm," The class hummed in harmony.

"I'm going to call it lemonade! And I am going to have a lemonade party at my farm!"

*****

Dear Diary – Bully

Cherry- Cheerleader, has to get good grades, popular but no one knows how lonely she is because everyone just wants to be her friend for popularity
Sander- Poor
Alex- Abusive, alcoholic parents
Chrissy- Parents missing, living with Grandmother
Celeste - Clicking noise of pencil, needs the noise to study, Perfume

Alex:

Dear Diary,
I'm not sure how to make today last forever but it has to. It's 11 o'clock at night and I should be sleeping. But it's the last day of summer break. The last day of peace and quiet. The last day of lying on my cushy carpet, ipod in hand, feet on my bed, undisturbed. I wish I could just stay here forever…Damnit, Dad's home….

Dear Diary,
Ohmigod Cherry is out of control with perkiness. She has the perfect little house with her perfect little car and perfect little clothes and she bounces around like the world is made out of cotton candy and polka dots. I think

if she gets in my face about… well, anything… I'm gonna flip.

Alright, maybe I'm just tired and cranky. Dad left the front door open again last night. I heard it slam against the coat rack and then everything fell off it at like 2am but as I crept down the stairs I saw Dads face first in the green rug. Sleeping. He must have found his way to bed eventually, I heard him leave for work this morning. No idea where he was but whatever.

Cherry:

Dear Diary,

Wow, this summer flew! I cannot believe everything that happened. Sorry I didn't write much, I just had so much fun in the sun and at camp! Jamie, Alex, Rollin, Sara, and I shared a bunk at cheer camp. The poor people next door probably didn't get any sleep. For some reason when you put us all together, we are obnoxiously loud. What a crazy month. It was like no one in the world could possibly be as close as we all became. Turns out Jamie kissed Scott, one of the counselors. Not even just one of the counselors, but the wicked hot swim instructor. Holy crap, his abs showed through his T-shirts. Anyway, Rollin finally overcame her fear of taking her clothes off in front of us in the locker room. She has these weird little round scars along her rib cage but we all told her it wasn't a big deal. She seems to be over the whole changing -under-a-tee-shirt thing for now. Those marks are really weird but whatever. Her long blond hair makes up for it. I would do anything for that hair. Ugh, this whole pulling out the iron at 5 am every morning to straighten my mop is getting pretty old. Maybe Mom will give me money to chemically straighten it again. Anyway, I am psyched to go back to school. I haven't seen anyone since camp, there is so much to talk about.

Oh, and did I mention there's a new guy in the neighborhood? I have no idea where he came from. He moved into the Flannigan's old place at the end of Stagecoach. But I haven't seen any parents or anything. Its just like a constant flow of people in and out. Anyway, he is super-hot. I re-routed my jogging path to pass by his house. Of course, this means I have to actually look good when I go jogging which is kinda hard when your sweating like a pig. I just got to run into him somehow... Ha! Listen to me, what a psycho! I don't even know how old he is! Okay, enough daydreaming, I really got to go to bed or I'm never gonna get up in time.

Dear Diary,

I'm not sure what happened but it seems like everyone kind of changed this summer. Not even just this summer, but like in the month since camp ended. We all had lunch together, but somehow our usual loud, attention drawing laughing kind of disappeared. Its like everyone wanted to be somewhere else. Or their minds were somewhere else. Jamie is dating a senior. She has been going to some crazy parties. Just today, I have heard more stories about drugs, alcohol, and sex than I care to share, let alone write down out of shear fear that someone sees this and she is damned to boarding school for the rest of the year. Alex was super weird. She said something about her parents keeping her up all night and being tired but she didn't want to talk. She just kind of stared at her apple. I think I'm gonna have a party or something on Columbus weekend. Get the squad back to the way we were.

Oh, classes were okay. Seem pretty easy. Miss Bradley seems like she is just going to give us a lot of essays and grade on how much we write so that should be an easy A. And the art teacher just lets people walk in and out of class whenever they want. Weird, but whatever. It should be a pretty easy year.

Dear Diary,

So cheerleading practice was a disaster. Rollin didn't even try. She kept picking at her fingernails. Then she declared that she would no longer be the flyer because she was afraid she was going to get dropped and never walk again. She has never been dropped but whatever, she is obviously more interested in keeping her boy toy happier than the squad. She is so stupid. After all we have worked for. We have states at the end of December and no one is small enough to take her place. Alex didn't even show up. I can never find her in the lunch room anymore either. We all made a point to match our schedules for this year so we had the same lunch period and now she is nowhere to be found. I don't know, I kind of feel like the squad is falling apart…

Dear Diary,

So I sent out an evite for the party next weekend. Dad said I could take the boat out as long as its only us girls so that will be fun. I think I'll make little rolls of turkey and cheese and maybe that microwave Chex mix. That's good boat food. Maybe we can have a bonfire or something too. The only bad thing is this stupid new girl at school decided she was going to have a party the same day and I saw that she sent out her invite, literally 12 minutes, after I did. Good luck New Girl, you are nothing. I think.

Dear Diary,
So I got the evite responses back from most of the girls… except Rollin said she wouldn't come unless she could bring that guy and convinced Anna that it is going to be lame with just us so now she wants to have guys come too. This is not at all what I had in mind. And to make it even worse, I heard that if I don't let guys come, they are going to New Girl's party instead.

Dear Diary,
This party is going to be such a disaster. Everyone wants to bring a guy or another friend or something. Its actually turning into a really big party. Mom and Dad said they would go out for the night so I'm not going to tell them it didn't turn into just being girls because I know they would never allow that. And I can't stand to be upstaged by New Girl. I'm not really feeling up to this at all but whatever. I can't cancel it now. I am the only one who ever throws parties worth going to and I can't lose that title. And ever since word started to travel about it, I have become like the center of conversation and social life at school. Its kind of nice to be miss popularity again. I mean, I definitely missed it over the

summer! The squad may make complete fools of ourselves at states but at least I'll still be captain. And popular.

Dear Diary,
So the party is this weekend. And I'm super stressed about it. I heard that James got his older brother to buy a keg to bring. Like, a whole keg. No one asked me if it was okay but Chris kind of mentioned it in passing. I had to keep a straight face and not appear shocked or anything. I don't want the whole football team thinking they are going to get caught partying at my house and then not come. Or even worse, I don't want them to think that I am worried or anything. Ugh, what am I saying, I'm not even supposed to have guys here for the party. I really hope this doesn't turn into a complete disaster.

Dear Diary,
You ever notice that when a lot of people envy you and want to be you, they talk bad behind your back? Its like, if you want to be like me, why wouldn't you say good things about me? I guess it never used to bother me when the squad was really close but I heard Rollin mocking me… I know her life kind of sucks compared to mine but it's not my fault.

*****

Jack and Jill

Jack and Jill were married under very interesting circumstance. Jack, the son if a very peculiar individual, known for climbing castle walls, only to fall from them, crack his skull, and simply repeat the same ridiculous action once he was cured. Unfortunately, one fall was from a rather high wall and despite the best efforts of all the kings' horses and all the kings' men, he could not be put back together again. Jack, inevitably inherited some of his father's clumsiness. He was not exactly safe to be around, as he was always causing himself and other around him a great deal of harm. This was not to terrible at first, not until his father was gone did Jack begin to feel very alone.

Jill, on the other hand, was a very empathetic person by nature. She understood what being alone felt like. Jill was born with a terrible malady which caused her nose to grow every time she lied. This not only made her relatively unattractive, but also inspired a candidness which many found to be offensive. Because of this, she spent much time alone. That was, until she met Jack.

The two were wed in late spring at the precise moment the cow jumped over the moon and the little stars began twinkle-twinkling. They exchanged vows at a private ceremony in their back yard, shaded by the rolling hills to the west.

Jack and Jill lived very happily together… mostly. But they faced one serious dilemma. The well from which they were to draw their water, was situated at the very peak of the very highest hill to the west. And every time that they tried to fetch water, Jack would inevitably fall over, with his pail of water, tumbling several feet before crashing into Jill, sending her tumbling after. The neighbors were aware of this issue and would usually come to their rescue, bandaging their wounds and fetching the water for them that they would need for the week. Really, all problems could be avoided by simply asking for help in the first place but both were so timid and ashamed of their lack of coordination that they never dreamed of asking anyone for assistance.

One day, while sitting around the fire, sipping wine (as they had to ration their water supply and wine was easily purchased from the vineyard) Jill decided to take a stand. She no longer felt like having her bones broke and tearing her skin, or depending on the neighbors for help; she knew they needed a long-term solution. They needed a source of water that would be available on demand. They needed something convenient, something to be kept in the house and produced on demand. They needed something with a lot of water… they needed a snowman!

The next morning, encapsulated in bandages and feeling only slightly better than the day before, the two headed out.

"Where are we going to find a snowman?" Jack demanded of Jill? Jack was not as happy about Jill's solution to their water issue but he could find no other alternative. He had no opinion to offer and so he kept quiet and went along. Jill was all he had, after all.

"Well, where would you be if you were a snowman?"

"In a bar, drinking my pathetic life away, avoiding those crazy children that planted me in a front yard in the middle of suburbia hell."

"Look, Jack, if you want to stay here and be miserable and thirsty all by yourself than stay, see if I care." The rise of volume in her voice told Jack that this was not the time to be messing around and he should probably just go along with her. "Wait, Jack that's it!" she cried. "A front lawn! That's where we will find a snowman!"

They had heard of these great big houses near Neverland. They felt fairly confident that a large house would mean a large snowman. They set off into the 100 Acre woods in complete silence. Ever since the most recent fall down the hill, Jack and Jill were not getting along so well. Hours passed as they strode along until Jack tripped on something, nearly sending him flying into Jill again.

"Damn it, Jack! Could you try not to injure me, for once!"

"Wait, I tripped over something, really!" Jack knelt down and felt around for the culprit. What he found was a young, dark haired beauty lying on the ground, fast asleep.

"Excuse me ma'am?"

No reply.

"Excuse me but I believe this is a rather dangerous place to lie your head. It is a relatively busy trail, ya know."

Nothing.

Jack got closer to her to examine this stillness.

"Good grief! I think she is dead!" Jack felt for her pulse and instinctively put his lips to hers to begin CPR. Upon this initial contact, though, the young girl opened her eyes.

"It worked! I'm so good, I should be a doctor!"

Jill stood in astonishment that her newlywed husband had put his lips near another woman's mouth.

"Oh, dear, where am I? What happened?"

Jack recounted the events for her and helped her to her feet. "My name is Sleeping Beauty, what's yours?"

"Oh, for the sake of holy donuts! That's your name?" Jill rolled her eyes." What kind of name is that? You aren't sleeping anymore and you could certainly use a little Maybelline." she continued under her breath.

The girl slid on her glass slippers and climbed to her feet.

"We were just headed out to find a snowman if you would like to join us!" Jack said, almost pleadingly. He was sick of the grumpy tension with his wife and had instantly found himself very enamored by this woman.

Jill shot him a glance signifying she was not in any mood to entertain but Jack found himself ignoring her for the first time in a very long time.

And so, the three continued on their way. Sleeping Beauty had no idea where she was or how she got there but she, like Jack, had fallen almost instantly in love with this fine new person and wanted to continue on with them.

Jill, growing more and more annoyed as the minutes passed, began to pick small fights with Jack. That night as they all laid their heads down to rest, Jill decided to tell Jack exactly how she felt.

"Fine! You can kiss girls all you want but I'm going to kiss…" she looked all around. "this frog!" She plucked the green creature from its cozy shelter and smooched him right on the lips. Low and behold the ugly frog turned into a Prince. Jack was in shock ….

*****

Jar of Hearts (song writing)

I learned to live, half alive and now you want me one more time.

But half alive is no way to live.

I don't need to push myself down, belittle myself, my beliefs, my passions, become only a small part of myself, the part you like, just to please you.

I did it for a while but that little while was long enough, too long.

I lost that time to a person who didn't even know the real me.

And now you want me to do it again? Now you want me back?

No, you don't, you only want half of me back.

You want the half of me that you know, that I let you see, that I didn't mask to please you and be what you wanted. Its not your fault, you never asked me to be perfect, I just thought I had to be.

I thought that pleasing you was the way to please myself.

But I was not happy then, so I won't do it again.

Loneliness

Loneliness might be one of the most tragic emotions visible in another person. An emotion that instills such an empathetic reaction in yourself, it is as if you are the subject of the emotion yourself. To stand apart from the person, at distance, knowing that there is not actually anything that you can do. Because those lonely people have created such a place for themselves, isolating their entire beings, pushing others out. There is no part of them that can keep that person from pushing you out. Just like all the others before you. Because, do not vainly believe that you are the only one to care. The only tried and true empathic, sympathetic, and emotionally devoted person to ever attempt to help this person. You aren't. it isn't you. it's them. And they have created this pocket woven in the fabric of the world. You can choose to move on.

******

She had recently fallen in love with this idea of the classy, sophisticated era of the 50's. When women only stepped out of their houses in dresses, freshly pressed and strategically coordinated to their shoes. Hair coiffed into a perfect assembly of gentle waves or finger curls carefully placed and topped with the daintiest of hat, often a piece of feather artfully dripped off the side, shielding a small fraction of her face. A subtle, yet demure suggestion of the sexual being masked behind the tailored proper exterior. She admired the way people once regarded travel, not as an inconvenience, any excuse to don this most comfortable pair of leggings or sweats. But rather, a time when people saw a day of travel as a privilege, and half of the adventure. When men would wear suits and overcoats. Women equally adorned. Travel as viewed as an occasion, not a means to an end.

As she arrived in Albany International Airport, a small, 3 wing establishment, in fact smaller than the local high school, only considered international as it made one daily trip to Quebec, a mire 45-minute trip by plane, she sipped her skinny vanilla latte and couldn't help but to judge her fellow travelers. Fully aware that it was no longer 1950, and such fashions would be hard to obtain, let alone pull off without appearing in costume for a Mary Poppins theatrical performance, it was hard not to look down upon the state of the attire surrounding her. Sure, it was just before 7 AM, and most of these people probably had needed to crawl out of bed much earlier than their usual time. But she had managed to drag herself out of bed, from beneath the arm of the only man she would ever love, in the once – every- two- weeks-if – she -was – lucky embrace.

She had managed to pull herself together quite nicely. Putting more attention into her outfit then most work days. And was even braving the freshly snow-covered sidewalk with 3 inch heels. Because, as her mother had taught her only too recently, that's what ladies do. And she had only too recently decided that she was a lady. At 29, she had only begun to actually figure out who she really was. As cliché as that sounds it was the first time that she chose a persona for herself, and was working to make herself such.

Taking cues from Marilyn Monroe, she cut 8 inches from her fine, yet abundant blonde locks, leaving a shoulder length layered style perfectly prepared to be curled and sprayed into that 50s style, but also reasonable enough to be left today into simple straight, yet adult–ish look. She took to lining her lips in a petal pink, or bold red, and filling the part with lipstick. Not a strawberry flavored lip gloss, free with a $50 purchase at a Victoria's Secret, but an actual tube of color lipstick. She even purchased a tailored pant suit from what was considered an upper – income ladies clothier. She felt elegant in said pant suit and chiffon blouse, gold earrings, enough gold bracelets to make a statement, without appearing gaudy, and a gold and crystal drop necklace, framed between her distinct collar bones and chiffon shirt collar.

As she walked the halls of the airport, she knew she drew attention, not just because of the deep clap her every step made with her wooden sale heels made, but also because of how she carried herself – with class and poise. More than once, she had been told that she was incredibly poised, confident, some even considered her, or rather assured her, to be conceited, based upon how the way she walked, smiled, or some other attribute she had yet to figure out. Because in all reality, confidence was not something she felt at all. In fact, her life was stark proof of this. So much so, that she was a bit disrespectful of her health and body, accepting men whom others considered beneath her, even when men themselves considered themselves beneath her. Sometimes abusing her health and safety in the interest of winning others appreciation or approval.

But nonetheless, she still found herself silently judging the travelers around her. Wondering whether the plaid pajama pants were really necessary for a two-hour flight. Did they realize they were in public? And while they were in the air, people 20,000 feet below were starting their day in real clothing. What had they planned on doing upon arrival, changing into real clothes to start their own day? Their vacation? It all just seemed so illogical. And when she once again removed herself from the crowd in the waiting area by gate B6 to use the ladies room, she could feel hundreds of eyes on her. She could feel a man glancing from the top of her shoulders to her ankles. Often returning to her naturally round behind, only accentuated by her posture in heels. Are others taking in the fullness of her chest, enhanced by the silhouette of her hourglass figure. And women with their eyes following a similar pattern. Yet she wasn't sure how many were staring all of envy, appreciation, or perhaps wondering the purpose behind such a put together substance of formality. But it didn't matter. What mattered was that she turned heads. And that she meant she wasn't destined for a life of eternal single doom .... yet.

*****

I want you to get swept up in me. That, "wow you look like an angel in this sunlight, but I can't tell you that " way. That way when you want to be playful chasing me across the field and tackle me in a friendly fun tickling roll that leaves me laughing and screaming at the same time. I know it's in there. But is it in there for me? Are we too far gone? Have you lied to me too much to let that openness free? Afraid of what you might let out?

Am I too guarded, knowing there with you, every action has an equal if unpleasant reaction?

I want you to adore me, to mean what you say, admire me. Be truthful when you tell me I look stunning?
I want you to look at me like you won the lottery. Not like I'm a chore.

*****

Million Dollar Game

His eyes instinctively squinted against the glaring Manhattan sun. Was it really still daytime? He had been in the studios so long, he had subconsciously expected to enter the same dim, artificially lit world he had just left. This wasn't how he envisioned today going. He thought he would arrive for his 1pm appointment, audition, whatever they call it when you are being interviewed for a reality show. It wasn't really acting, right? It was a showcase of your real life. Why the casting director had thought he might be the perfect candidate for The Weightless Challenge was beyond him. Why would a former college Division 1 lacrosse player need to lose weight? Sure, his muscle definition wasn't at its prime, recent mass amount of beer intake had certainly begun to install love handles, but he still fit into a pair of 36/34s and wasn't spilling over his board shorts. But maybe that was the problem.

His application looked good. Former college athlete-turned-loan manager. From running fields to running numbers. Rock solid abs to white-collar paper pusher. Recently heartbroken, looking for massive changes in his life. Ready to relocate to the West Coast, ready to relocate anywhere, really. It sounded like the perfect intro to the newest reality show slated to grace the small screen next fall. It sounded like a perfect opportunity to escape the small town that seemed to be sucking the life from his withering spirits.

They were lucky he even answered the phone. Most unknown numbers were bill collectors or telemarketers, which he ignored. True, he was in the banking industry, but his student loans, backed by lofty dreams, had haunted him since graduation, perpetuated by his irrational need to buy Jenna's love. Freddie Mac had taken a backseat to Jenna Monroe. Roses favored to loans. He knew from his current work training that credit card payments affected a credit score in exponential ways compared to student debt. Coach tote, sure. That pair of Louis Vuitton pumps you have lusted over for years, no problem. A trip to Seychelles, why not? He found himself recently wishing he had taken those pumps from the box they never left, wrap them up in the tote she never used, and shove them up that perfectly sculpted ass he was never allowed to use. Bitch.

But he did answer the phone. Part of him thought it might be Jenna calling. Begging for forgiveness, ready to confess her undying love and promising a life full of sobriety and babies- a desire for the white picket fence and loving husband. Part of him was simply having a crappy day and felt like venting- the bill collector being a perfect target. Those people were used to it. And who willingly takes those jobs unless they have some weird mental deformity that allows them to listen to bullshit lies and the click of an untimely hang-up hundreds of times a day? Regardless, he didn't have anything better to do that afternoon. His day off had consisted of day-drinking Magic Hat #9 and watching reruns of Hoarders on TV. When he answered, he was ready for a fight, the fight or flight response already flooding his veins with adrenaline.

Which is why he was taken so aback when the high-pitched voice of a young-sounding woman asked for Dillon Tate. Informing him that she was calling him from Anecdote Studios and confirming his identity. He was wary. Was this for real? He vaguely remembered applying to their reality show casting call online only two nights ago. He wasn't entirely sure what he had included on the application. The cheap rum from his homemade mojitos clouding his judgement and providing liquid courage to step out of his current situation. Would they want to ask him questions? Confirm his application responses? What if he lied? While he listened to the hold audio pre-recorded trailers for the latest shows, he desperately powered on his computer and waited for Windows to open. He silently cursed himself for opting for the cheap Dell over the MacBook he really wanted, those things were almost instant. You're welcome, Jenna. Hope your Zappos page loads in a matter of seconds. He had just managed to open a new browser when a deep male voice broke through the trailers.

"Mr. Tate?" The voice sounded far away.

"Uh, yes?"

"Hello Mr.Tate, my name is Robert Sonden, I am the executive producer of the Weightless Challenge. I have you on speaker with my casting director, Ally Fields." He paused. "Mr.Tate? You applied online for our reality show casting?"

He was still trying to pull up his application, and had only half heard what he said. "Uh, yeah, call me Dillon."

"Mr.Tate, Dillon, you sound like someone we might be interested in meeting, would you mind us asking a few questions?" Robert Sonden sounded very official, serious. Not at all like the gum chewing park-trash he had expect a call to be from- either of the people he expected a call from.

"Yeah, sure." He couldn't access the answers he had submitted, but was able to find the questionnaire application and began skimming the questions, racking his brain for some memory of what he had written.

"You mentioned that you played Lacrosse professionally. Could you elaborate on that, Mr. Tate?" Shit, he had lied. Why wasn't there a breathalyzer on computers? Or phones for that matter. "As far as we could see, your name was not listed on any of the major league rosters."

Lying was not his strong suit. He left that to Jenna. That girl could think on her feet faster than OJ Simpson's lawyer. "I, uh, I played D1 college lacrosse. I was drafted, but I decided on a different path." Well, there, that wasn't a lie. He had been drafted. He had chosen a different path. Not that he would have ever made it very far. Lacrosse just happened to be something he was good at, not something he loved. He followed his heart. Stupid.

"Oh, we thought," there was some whispering and a long pause, "would that other path have anything to do with this girl you mentioned?"

Oh for the love of God, how much detail had he gone into on that damn application? How did he even manage to type that much? Sometimes he wondered how he even got himself to bed at night, only to find that he had cleaned the entire loft and managed to make his lunch for the next day. Maybe he should drink all day, too. Productivity seemed to be directly proportional to his alcohol consumption. "You mean Jenna?"

"Uh, if that is the official name of 'the blood-sucking-leach' then I guess yes, we are speaking of Jenna. What is her last name Mr.Tate? Er, Dillon?"

Well, there was no point in hiding the truth now, he had apparently laid his entire life out for Hollywood, there was no turning back now. And so the questions began. "Jenna. Her name is Jenna Monroe."

"Dillon, nice to see you again." Finally, someone dropped the formalities. Mr. Tate was his father. Dillon was most certainly not his father, and would prefer not to be referred to that way. "I'll show you to the green room." Ashley was pretty typical for what he expected for an LA assistant. Tall, leggy, blonde. A little bohemian vibe from the looks of her flowing floral dress. It was almost a relief to have something happen the way he envisioned it. Her. The last few weeks had been a blur, an act. His whole life had become a performance, preparing for the ultimate change of circumstance. After all, he was going to be dead in a matter of hours.

Dillon still hadn't fully accepted the decision that he had made. He was most certainly not a heartless animal, void of empathy and compassion. In fact, he fancied himself quite the opposite. He teared up at funerals. Defended the pudgy kids in school. He was never the "leader of the pack" in school. Not because he wasn't popular enough. In fact, with his reputation and incredible athletic prowess, he could have run his school. Any school. But he could never get into the heartless ignorance many of his teammates exhibited. He hadn't always been a star athlete, a D1 star. He wasn't born with rich parents, doting over his every move, and enrolling him in top-notch athletic camps. And he held on to that. Part of him even felt a little bad for Jenna. Though she had ripped his heart straight from his chest, scraping it through his ribs, cracking them and causing jagged tears on the way out, part of that heart felt for her.

"I stocked the mini-fridge with some of your favorites. And there are Quest bars, popcorn, and sugar-free vanilla wafers in the cabinet. I couldn't get Stewarts chocolate chip cookies right away, but the shipment should arrive by the end of the week."

"Wait, what?" He was confused. Pleased, but confused. How did boho-blonde Ashley know what he ate? "Are you stalking my pantry?"

"Well, that is kind of why we are here." She smirked and walked across the room to the knotty-pine coffee table where an iPad was resting. "The cameras. They are all over your apartment, remember?" She pressed the home button on the iPad and unlocked it. Opening an app, and tapping on the screen with her perfectly pink nails, the 6 televisions on the wall flickered to life. Dillon hadn't even noticed them until now. "I also noticed you have a lot of knotty-pine and leather sofas, we weren't able to locate exact replicas, but I hope this makes you feel a bit more comfortable.

Ashley moved about the room gracefully, checking flashing lights on receiver boxes, testing fluently from her iPhone. Though she brought a small relief of calm, a somewhat familiar face to this tumultuous world, Dillon still struggled with accepting her as friendly. Though her movements were calm and intentional, there was something business-like about how she spoke to him. She wasn't overly friendly. She wasn't particularly warm. And Dillon had to remind himself that she wasn't a friend. He didn't have any of those anymore. He was about to die, and leave them here to suffer his choices. As he stood in the open doorway, he could see the glowing exit sign at the end of the hall, and he thought briefly of excusing himself and never coming back.

"There is a restroom for your convenience right here. Don't worry, there aren't any cameras in there. But when you come in each day, you will be expected to remain here for the duration, which will mean you need to stay in the room at all times. Mr.Sonden will be down in just a minute with the technician to run you through some more details and test the lighting and cameras. You will also meet Maliya, your hair and makeup artist. Due to the confidentiality of the situation, you will be seeing her quite a bit. She will be working with you, and only with you, for the duration." The duration, the word echoed in his head. She kept calling it the duration. The duration of your heartless, selfish, egocentric reality show was what she was probably thinking. "As for me, I am also assigned to your show, exclusively. If there is anything you need, please call." She glanced to the phone situated directly center of the coffee table. It was ornate, vintage almost, and had no buttons. How had he not noticed it before? "The line will dial directly to my cell when you pick it up. Same as your apartment."

As she was finishing her sentence, a stout man in a gray suit, top button undone and Maui-Jim sunglasses peeking out his pocket entered. "Mr.Tate," Mr.Sonden greeted in a lighthearted, just-stepped-off-my-yacht voice, "How are we doing today?"

"I'm alright." Tate replied, automatically. Not that he was alright. In fact, in that moment, the reality of his situation smacked him like a two-by-four in the face. Behind Sonden came two men, in khakis and RPE-embroidered polos, Reality Production Entertainment provided uniform, undoubtedly. They walked past Tate silently, immediately going to work on entering codes in boxes beside each of the televisions, peering into viewfinders of cameras situated beneath each one. Cameras were everywhere in this room. Behind the wet-bar, at least 5 to a wall. It seemed a bit excessive, given the close proximity of this 125 square foot room. One of them pulled out an archaic looking box and started fiddling with the switches. A few of the cameras began moving, scanning the room, which the other tech held a laptop and nodded succinctly, verifying the view each captured.

"This is Maliya. She will be making you beautiful. Well, as beautiful as that sullen mug of yours is going to get," Sonden chuckled briefly at his own joke, casting a glance to Ashley, who dutifully smirked back. Maliya was also what he expected, in the brief moments he had to conjure up a preconceived notion of a Hawaiian makeup artist. She was petite, 5'3" at best. Much different than Ashley. Though employed as a makeup artist for a major production company, she was not particularly made-up. Her features defined by light eyeliner, her hair coiffed into a neat bun, off her face. But still, she was pretty. And seemed timid. She didn't speak, but rather just nodded her head in greeting.

"Maliya will be in every few hours. Camera lighting can be very unforgiving, and we want to be sure you look your best. But she has a passkey. She will let herself in. If it is a bad time, you can ask her to step out. We understand you may not always be up for company. We just ask that you allow her in a few times each day, and most importantly, that you do not talk to her."

"You don't want me to talk to her?" Dillon asked her, a bit insulted.

"Dillon, this is your show, no one else's. We want to capture the reality of your situation. Maliya is not part of the production, we wouldn't want to miss an opportunity to film your thoughts. And we cannot do that while you are being powdered and combed." Dillon acknowledged with a half-nod. His initial reality- check was now being replaced with a feeling of discomfort. Now he was being told who he could talk to?

"While we are on the subject, anyone who has permission, or reason, to enter this room will have a passkey. We ask that you not answer the door for any reason. If someone is permitted to enter, they will let themselves in. And with the exception of Maliya, Ashley, and myself, you will know ahead of time if anyone else will be stopping by."

Tate looked around them. It seemed as though it was his turn to speak. But this was all becoming overwhelming. So many people, so many rules, so much attention. But Sonden wasn't finished yet. "While we are on the subject, we would ask that you not speak to anyone, at all. Besides myself, or Ashley, of course. There are a lot of people who would like to know what we are working on in here. Once the teaser trailers start, there is no telling the lengths people will go to. So, as part of the contract states, you are not to speak to anyone. That means you do not open this door for anyone. I hope you understand, as a breach of contract, would also result in your… losing the competition."

Ah, yes, the contract. Tate remembered "The Meeting." The day he signed his life away, literally.

"Mr. Tate, welcome!" Half a dozen men were situated around the large board room table. "We are so happy you have chosen to join the RPE team." Team, ironic. He was acting as anything but a teammate right now. He was a backstabbing, selfish money-hungry maniac right now. But after last night's Facebook prowl, he was fueled by emotion. No one mattered. Nothing mattered. Apparently, he didn't even matter.

"Thank you, me too." Sonden's assistant motioned for him to sit and placed a sugar-free Red Bull and bottled water before him. His daily drink du-jour.

"I hope your flight was pleasant." Sonden didn't wait for a reply, "This is our board of directors, Craig Rochefort- Executive director, Benjamin Bradley- Director of Production, Ralph Mooreshouse- Director of Human Resources, Brian Landgraf- network legal consultant, Brian Moquin- network attorney, and, of course, William Pennock- Vice President of RPE." They stood, one-by-one, shaking his hand. "I know this may seem a bit overwhelming, but you have to understand the special circumstances surrounding such a production. Never has any network untaken such a drastic and dramatic endeavor. Thus… you could be groundbreaking for the reality television revolution. We want to make sure there are no questions left unanswered, no stones left unturned."

"Uh, should I have a lawyer here?"

The suited men chuckled. "Mr.Tate, please rest assured that we have nothing but your best interest at heart."Sonden spoke for the group. Dillon couldn't help but snort at the irony. Best interest. Ha. They were about to have him buried six feet under.

"Mr. Tate, if you are ready, we would like to go over the details of production." Craig paused. Dillon waited. "Mr. Tate, we are going to fake your death. As we have already discussed, we are going to use your prior head injuries and concussions as a cause of complications and subsequently your demise." He glanced up. Dillon was unmoved. He knew this already. It made sense that he would die as a result of a lacrosse injury. And it would be easier that way. His family could accept that. It would be shocking, but not unreasonable. Not traumatic like a drunk driving accident. While that would be entirely reasonable. He knew production was trying to limit the cost, and risk, of including the news and law-enforcement. It would cost a lot to stage all of that. Even more to pay off the stations to run such a report. "We will make it appear as though you went to the hospital with an extreme headache and have the doctors pronounce you dead after a brief stay".

The sounds of an ambulance echoing between buildings is unmistakable, as anyone in any big city could tell you. The ebbing sound seems to flow in waves, radiating louder and softer, accompanying the brash blinding lights spinning on the rooftop of the speeding vehicle. But in the greater cities of the United States, the vehicle is often left gridlocked, the radiating music of its siren stopped still in its tracks, every beat a symbolic reminder of the heartbeat fading within its shell.

The medics had tightened the straps a little too tight. The tension in the weaving vehicle increasing exponentially with each revolution of every light. The cliché idea of death tells us that one's life flashes before their eyes in their final minutes. In these minutes, flashes were more like glimpses, mini-movies, whether imagined or constructed: Dillon's first glimpses of light, a doctor, nurses, what seemed like an army poking and prodding, wiping and washing, preparing this tiny body for his first photo shoot, swaddled tightly beneath layers of blue and pink striped cotton, a tiny beanie hat sealing in the heat rapidly escaping this tiny body, used to the warmth of a mother's womb; and then to a couch, tiny hands grasping the soft brown fibers of a cushion, legs bouncing in a dance-like rhythm before repositioning his feet and releasing one hand, then another, and taking a daring step, free of outside supports, then another, before collapsing onto a diaper cushioned seat, giggling in exasperation; next a soccer field, a child, Dillon, his face buried in his mother's flowy green tunic, tears soaking the shirt, creating a heart-shaped shadow of social anxiety, this boy- terrified of the crowd gathered for the team's first-and-only game of the season; then a girl, a slender, blonde, teenage girl dressed in a long emerald gown, fitted to her knees, with a mermaid train, tenderly adjusting her wrist corsage, and smiling the smile of a girl who was the luckiest girl on earth, glancing only once to meet the eyes of her date, blonde ringlets tossing in the breeze, strands sticking to her lip gloss as she gently slid them away; and then drifting to the last lacrosse game of Dillon's career, bleachers packed on both sides, students dressed in emerald and gold, layers

105

of students pressing against one another, forcing the front row against the fences, homemade signs in hand, cheering Dillon and his team, parents secretly praying for their sons, girlfriends encouraging their boyfriends, unaware of the implications of a semi-pro recruitment, completely unaware that this may be the last time they see the one they love above all else. All aware of the implications. All unaware of the repercussions.

Carol Tate hadn't opened her eyes since she collapsed. A neighbor had come over for their weekly tea and, surprised by the lack of response, and driven by a well-known characteristic of nosiness, had let herself in. In all of her years of "snooping" Maureen had never found something so jarring to her best friend, her only true confidant, Carol Tate, was in a misshapen ball on the kitchen floor- seemingly collapsed from her chair, tea still steeping in the dainty porcelain pot she reserved for their Wednesday meetings. She helped her to her feet and led her to the car.

"Tate," was all she mumbled as her lashes fluttered against the blinding fluorescent bulbs of the ER.

"Carol, sweetie, Tate isn't here, Tate is gone, remember?" Maureen grasped Carol's hand in this moment, an un usual tenderness forced in her tone. Having pressed the nurse call button on the bed, Maureen had summoned the nurse entering the room, but hurried the words out before someone was able to stop her. The nurse, a young brunette, her tag reading nothing but S Austin, eyed her carefully. "His apartment, remember, we cleaned it out?"

"Ma'am, could you just step out to the waiting room, please?" The nurse was young and couldn't have more than a few years' experience under her belt, but she certainly had a knack for recognizing a meddler. Her stance was stern, defiant if necessary. She stood, body squared, in the direction of the meddler. "We will come and get you if we need anything."

Maureen stood tall from her crouched position, realizing that her typical well-poised stature had been sacrificed in a moment of weakness. She eyed her dear neighbor, the closest thing she had to a friend and then glanced back to the straight-faced nurse before heading toward the door. Maureen stopped just before leaving the room and turned on her heels, "Her name is Caroline. He did it all for her, and in the name of the woman he loved the most."

2008 – Short Story

Teresa Noel was a small girl. She was so small, in fact, that the snow nearly covered her head. She didn't mind this, of course, as she lived her entire life practically covered in snow. You see, Theresa lived in Winterville- a town almost as small as she was. Winterville, though it was small, was a hugely magical place. For here, it was almost always winter. And not just Florida winter, or the mild winters of California- North Pole winter. To some, this might seem horrible and miserable, but to Wintervillettes, it was perfect. Small twinkling lights adorned roofs all year and lined branches of the frozen trees of the village. It was never dark, never sad, and never, ever boring.

*****

This year, however, seemed a little different than past years. This year, however, was colder, had more snow (a lot more snow). Which was good for some but not Teresa Noel. You see, the snow had gotten so high and out of control that Teresa had become invisible! She had gone on her family's monthly tree-trip and had to be carried around on the top of the tree after her father almost stepped on her! She had to walk on a rolling snowball to get to school... unfortunately by the time she got there the snowball was taller than the school and she couldn't get in!

"Don't be a humbug," her father would say, "you are perfect." The problem was, it was hard to be perfect when you weren't even visible. And Teresa had had enough.

It was the night before Christmas and everything was still. Everyone was sleeping, except Teresa Noel. She filled her pillowcase with the necessities (a brush, sweater, toys) and set out in search of a place she could be seen for who she was. After all, no one could see her here- she certainly wouldn't be missed. With no plan and no map, armed only with a lamp to melt the way, Teresa wandered through that night and as she approached the edge of town, she noticed how dark the world was. For the first time in her life, she was not surrounded by cheer, glitter, and twinkling lights. But it was also the first time that she could see clearly for miles without a snow bank obstructing her view. Any fear or remorse she felt was replaced by her excitement for a new life- a life where she was someone. *~still working here~*

Hallow Queen's Town was dark, very dark, all the time. The streetlights resembled jack-o-lanterns with faces that changed from happy to sad to scared and scary. Through the clenched teeth of the terrifying lanterns came a dull resonance of moans and cries. There were no sleighs drawn through the snow but rather rotten piles of leaves clogging the drains and crunching beneath the feet of ghosts as they coasted through the streets. As Teresa approached the door of The Spider Cove in, she felt this was no longer the place she thought it would be.

The door swung open to reveal a haggard old woman with hair springing from her ears. The rats surrounding the old woman quickly rushed forward to sniff their new guest's toes.

~ That's all I got for now... not sure which direction I want to take it..

■■■ ■■

<u>Diary of a Hot-mess</u> (fictional short story)

4/28/15

I started writing in my diary for therapy and some self-reflection. It helped me a lot and I hope it encourages others to do the same.

I'm not sure when it all started, perhaps back in college. Maybe the company I kept, or the party girl life I led. I thought I was invincible, I did whatever I wanted and enjoyed every part of life. But I did have limits – no drugs, no drinking and driving, and no smoking! What's left you ask? Drinking. It seemed like there was always a party, always a reason – It was easy and fun.

I've been dating Dean for almost a year now, I thought he may be "the one". We started a business venture together but I found myself doing most of the work. Although I have to confess I do enjoy any excuse to spend time outside and landscaping challenged me physically as well as taught me how to do things I would never had done.

Well that's enough of the introduction, you will soon learn enough about me and the challenges I will be faced with.

3/17/15

This journal book is so perfectly new, it has sat on my table for over two weeks. I felt unworthy of it or something, it is beautifully bound and perfect. But since I made my 30 in 30 list last night, and committed to writing 30 minutes a day, and have felt zero inspiration lately, what better time to start a journal. Maybe it will be therapeutic. Or maybe it will just be fun to look back at in the years to come. Or maybe something tragic will happen to me and this will either provide some solace for loved ones left behind, or evidence for some crime investigation. Who knows. But, hey, that's a good story idea.

Part of me was also considering giving this journal to Dean. He mentioned once before wanting to write – as kind of a therapy. But I knew it would probably end up as a drink coaster. He respects nothing nice. He says he does, but actions speak louder than words. He spent Friday night here with me telling me he wants to be with me, only me, only for "Emily" to text him "Enjoy your night and have fun at the parade tomorrow". That was enough to decide the journal is mine. Dr. Carlson says I just keep letting things happen to me. I guess she's right. I couldn't even buy myself a nice journal. I had to wait for Dean to be undeserving of it. Am I ever going to be able to choose happiness? Or am I always going to be that bobber in the ocean?

Back to Dean (see here I go again). I was clearly annoyed Saturday after seeing the text from Emily, even if it's my own fault for reading it. So, I asked if he meant what he said last night. He said yes. I believed him. I texted "I love you". He replied, "I love you too". It was St. Patty's day in Albany and he went drinking all day. I was supposed to meet him after work. He didn't really want me to. I could tell by the two-hour delay between texts. So I didn't go. I didn't even want to go. I hate his friends, and there were probably drugs involved. Why did I even consider going? What is it about him that I love so much? Despite also having plans Sunday, I didn't hear from him until 6pm Sunday – just an explanation that he was hungover. Slacker. I didn't answer and I haven't heard anything since. He's probably sleeping with Emily. I'm too much work for him. My family. Staying clean. Being honest. I demand the best from him – maybe that's too much work. I got drunk at Sally's Sunday night, afterwards I cried and vented to my mom about how men don't want to be with me, then I went home.

I was so depressed yesterday, my eyes swollen, my face puffy – I'm sure I looked awful at work. But I felt bad enough to not drink. Let's try this again. Maybe if I can swear off men for 30 days, I can also not drink for 30 days. Today is day 2. Thirty days will be the tail end of spring break. I guess I'll see what happens then. If I last that long. I wish I could fall asleep easier. I just ordered a white noise machine. I hope that helps. I also ordered new pens. That will help me writing. Today is also day 2 of writing 30 minutes. I can do this. I wish I had bought this journal for my past soulmate that is now my angel. This is exactly what he wanted.

I'll just fill it for you Muffin xo

3/18/15

I am so tired today. I woke up in tears at 1:30am. I had a nightmare that Dean went to prison. I know why I had the dream. I pictured visiting him in prison. Hugging him and having him appreciate my hug for the first time. Wanting to stay in that place forever – his arms, not the prison. What I didn't know is why I had that image in my head in the first place. Why was I even picturing him in prison? Maybe I think that is the only place I could keep him away from anyone else? Because I can't be with him but I don't want anyone else to be either? Or is it because Dean makes me feel like I'm in prison? Am I overanalyzing myself? I do kind of feel like I do feel imprisoned by him. I love him so much and I am so hopeful for him. I want him to get better and believe he can and believe we can be so happy together. I find something wrong with anyone I meet. And they find something wrong with me. I can't escape this grasp he has on my heart. I don't want to. Which is ridiculous.

Drugs are a demon he will fight forever. Why am I fighting for a chance to fight with him? I have potential for happiness. Why can't I realize them in my heart? What if he is my soulmate? I know that sounds ridiculous. I almost texted him last night when I was in tears, I'm glad I didn't. He wouldn't have answered, or he would have. And he would have been loving and charming and wonderful. And I'd be ten steps back. Will this ever get easier? His birthday is Saturday. He didn't text me on my birthday. Will I be able to be so strong?

I am taking the County Civil Service exam on Saturday. It pays $45K/year. That sounds so little. Could I be setting myself up for a struggle again? Why does my life feel so difficult? Like I should have just gone to Boces for cosmetology. Who the hell knows.

Day 3 of no drinking. I wanted a glass of wine when I got out of work but when I got home it wasn't even a thought. I was more concerned with sleep. I was supposed to do some work for Prestige but last night wore me out. Sleep made me tired. I want warmer weather and the motivation to run. I want to keep not drinking. That's not going to be easy next weekend at the casino. I'm going to need to either decide not to drink or to drink and give up 12 days sober. If I make it that long. Wow, I say that a lot. I really need to get my perkiness back. I need to come up with a better way to answer, "How's it going?". Something better than "I'm alive". No wonder I don't have a job.

Today's photo (#2) my usually neat desk at work completely concealed in papers – a crazy day.

Three days no alcohol.

Today's reading: Nicholas Sparks "The Longest Ride"

3/19/15

It is strange that my greatest accomplishment is committing to writing 30 minutes and reaching 30 minutes a day. I mean, there are things I enjoy, why do I need to force myself to do them? Not that I'm forcing myself, but I am forcing myself to make time. Maybe its good tho. Maybe after 21 days it will become a habit. Maybe then I can start to actually write something productive. I was thinking to myself earlier that this writing was productive because it is like talking to a therapist every night. And I'm not whining to my best friend all the time. But since I started doing this I haven't been sleeping well. But maybe it isn't the writing. Maybe its still from alcohol withdrawal. I offered to drive Mom and her friends around Saturday, so that's good. A good reason not to drink. If I get through this weekend, I'll almost be at one week, and soon I'll pass my 10 day mark, which is the longest I have gone so far. It helps that I was so depressed Monday. I can't do that again.

Speaking of, Dean checked Facebook 18 minutes before last time I checked. It was kind of a relief. I wish I could say I was relieved to see he was alive, but really I think him being on FB meant he isn't with Emily. Who knows. I gotta get a friggin life. It definitely helped reading Nicholas Sparks last night – just like Twilight, it reminded me of how I wanted to be treated. It felt good – granted I'm not in the book. It was inspirational. I'm in a better place today, and I want to stay here. I am a good person. I work hard. I am honest. I deserve someone who appreciates that and can give what I give and wants to.

I'm glad I'm writing. I was so hesitant to defile this book, but the truth is, it looks better with my pretty script filling its tamed pages.

I think I need to start setting small attainable goals for myself daily. One's that are realistic and that I can make a plan for. My goal tomorrow is to walk for 30 minutes. If I wake up tired, and the gym is out of the question, I will walk around the school. Maybe I'll invite one of my co-workers to walk with me. Maybe I'll get Sally to walk at the gym with me. I should probably check my account status first. I will NOT drink tomorrow. I will wake up early, refreshed, and ready to tackle the civil service exam, just to keep my options open. I feel good about the test - I think I have exactly the kind of instinct, personality, and reasoning skills for the job.

Today's photo (#3) A photo of this book – because I'm proud of the progress I have made and the dedication I have found

4 Days and no alcohol

Today's reading: Nicholas Sparks "The Longest Ride"

"Don't' be critical of things you can't understand" – Bob Dylan

3/20/15

Well, I survived a week. Well, almost. One week ago today, Dean was just getting here. He was making a drink and I decided to have one too. We drank and laughed. We cuddled and talked. Talked so much that we barely paid attention to what was on TV. We compared how much we missed one another. We reminisced about all the conversations we had on the patio. We both confessed we missed one another and wanted to be together. Too bad I was the only honest one in the conversation. This led to the alcohol-fueled depression that lasted until Thursday. I have not answered his Sunday text, and I haven't heard from him since. I miss him. I think about him hourly. But it's getting better. It's getting easier. I think about him less. As long as I am busy. As long as I don't see any red pick-up trucks. His birthday is tomorrow. He didn't speak to me on mine. Hell, he is using the chest he made me as my belated present as a coffee table. Probably to do drugs on. Probably to hold his glasses of vodka. Why don't I hate him? Why did I just spend another page writing about him. I think there are too many unresolved things. I think I have left doors open for a reason. It scares me to close him out forever. I'm just not ready. I am ready to be happy. Maybe 30 days without booze or men is exactly what I need to do. Maybe. What I really need to do is focus my energy on me. On writing things I want to publish. On my civil service exam tomorrow. Although I'm not sure I can deal with $45K/year. Not when I have made more for doing less! I guess I don't need to decide anything right now. Just focus. On me. Tomorrow will be busy. Test, work, hair, Match event with mom, bond with friends. It will be busy. But good busy. I'm going to enjoy it. And I'm going to stay sober. And take a meaningful picture.

I didn't walk today, as I planned. But really, I was working so late. By the time I got home, it was wind-down time. I'm okay with that. Because this is just as important, if not more so. My mind needs to be calm. Healthy, if the rest of me is going to be good.

Today's photo (#4) is of my Valerian Root plant. I do not have a green thumb, but they seem to be growing well. This could be the beginning of a new hobby! I read for about two hours today. Nicholas Sparks, I love your love stories. I love losing myself in them.

5 Days sober.

3/21/15

Well, in 20 minutes it will be Sunday. The last time I was so drunk, I was left reeling in anxiety and sorrow. I'm so proud of myself. I went out with Mom to the mall, I had fun. And I didn't drink. I didn't want to. I was disappointed we weren't going out in a group. Sadly I won't be going to a Match event where I might meet my next great love. But everything happens for a reason. I was distracted enough to forget about Dean and forget his birthday is today. And then I saw a guy that looked a lot like Matt. I was too shy to talk to him but it didn't matter. It was a nice reminder of how life can be. And my spirits were lifted. I am going to try to make myself do this more often. Get out. Meet people. Live my last days of being 29. Not that I have to stop living after that. In fact, I am trying to remain aware of the fact that it just a number. I feel young. I am young!

It is crazy how out-of-whack my emotions can get. Just eight hours ago I was in a garage with running cars and no fresh air. I started to get a headache, probably from carbon monoxide. I started to think how it good it would be if I died that way because then it would be an accident and no one would have to feel bad – like they could have stopped it from happening. And now here I am – renewed and happy! I am really going to try to hold on to this. And help my girlfriend Beth do the same. I think she needs a best friend – I'll try to be that person for her. She will be my significant positive impact on someone. I also did my first random act of kindness today – I bought the sandwich and donuts for the women behind me at Dunkin Donuts.

Off to read now … 6 days sober!

3/22/15

Today was a different Sunday – but different in a good way. Beth and I went to the gym, then Chipotle, then grocery shopping. It was nice to have someone to do these things with. Someone to talk to – who listens. Her kind-of boyfriend met us at the gym. He was hot. A little strange, very serious, but he was nice. I hope it works out for them. She deserves someone like him. I think he makes her want to be a better person. Maybe sometimes it is good to change for someone I guess.

On another note, I am going to be very sore tomorrow! I didn't even dwell on Dean, although I did tell Beth a lot of the background of what went down with Dean. I know I can trust her. And I think it helped us both because she is dealing with the same thing with her sister. She is addicted to heroin too. It is so sad how this has gripped the lives of so many people. Beth is afraid, or rather just waiting, for her sister to overdose or die. So sad. I'm glad I have been able to turn my life around. 7 days sober. I feel great. I really felt great working out. I'm getting my life back! I didn't take a picture today. Well I did take a couple screen shots of a guy on Match that I messaged. One of a recipe that is now cooking. Good enough. Off to write a little more and read.

3/24/15

Well, I missed a day of writing. But not because I was too lazy or too drunk or something, but because of a water main brake in my apartment complex and I had to stay at my parents. I brought my journal with me but didn't feel comfortable taking it out. I didn't want my mom knowing that I have this and go snooping to try to find it and read it, she's done that before. Yesterday was another good day. I went to the gym. I did legs and ran two miles on the incline. I'm so incredibly sore today, I took the night off. It was late anyway, after I tutored. I did talk to Dean today. I asked for money for the mower and trailer. I had invested into his new venture – landscaping – hoping this would set him on track. He didn't have the money. He said he could have it Tuesday. After some cold texts from me, I finally told him how I felt about him not inviting me out Saturday,

Emily's text, no word from him on Sunday. Surprisingly he was honest (I think) and told me he ran into Emily one night but nothing happened and his truck was repossessed and now he owes $1400 to get it back. He said he has never been so stressed and that he wants to get himself together before he can be back in my life. I know its dumb but I felt better. I still have him. And he says he is clean. He was drinking but I suggested he come to the gym with me and get the endorphins high. He seemed excited. We'll see.

On another note, I finished my first book last night – The Longest Ride – I loved it. I started reading "The Best of Me" but I am pretty sure I already read it, so I'm back to "Dirty Rush", which I thought I lost. Speaking of – 9 days sober! I feel amazing. Except for the terrible soreness – but that's gym soreness – and a sign I'm getting my summer body back – Yay! I also had a thought about my career today. A parent confided in me that her daughter is depressed and cutting. I felt awful for her. But I felt something else too. I felt an insatiable desire to help. I know I should have stuck with psychology. I looked into the programs at SUNY. I'm considering it. I'm still young, right? I suppose if it is meant to be, I'll figure it out. I already read for a while but not long enough to have heavy eyes, so back to the book I go.

3/25/15

Today was rough – ok, it wasn't all together rough but I had a little anxiety attack over not being able to find a classroom for professional development, so I hid in a bathroom and almost started crying. But I pulled myself together and asked for help. That is an accomplishment in my eyes and I'm actually proud of myself.

But then I picked up Dean and took him to Troy to take pictures. I love being around him. I'm talking to him. He has to come up with $1400 by next Friday or he can't get his truck back. While we were in the car, he admitted to doing some crazy drug that he got from that same guy. Why can't he stop getting in his own way?! My way! As much as I enjoyed his company, I felt no desire to go upstairs to his apartment when I dropped him off. To that, I am also proud. I held my guard up a little. Admittedly, it was easier because he was being so sweet and lovable. I felt secure, so I was able to walk away. I did give him $50 for coming – half of what I'll get paid for taking the pictures. I hope he doesn't buy drugs. God, please help him. Help me to not enable him. But really, if he loses his truck, that would be such a huge set back. I'm torn. But I'm sober – 10 days today! And I read almost two hours for work. And wrote a very reflective piece about anxiety. I feel like I'm getting a grip on myself. Finally! But then there's Dean. I hope getting him to go to the gym with me helps him. I wonder if I had the ability to know the future if I would really want to. Maybe I'll hit a jackpot this weekend and be able to help him. I'll definitely pay GMC directly though. Or not. Decisions aren't my strong suit.

3/26/15

Today was a pretty normal day. I went to work and it was PJ day, so I wore yoga pants and a hoodie. I was supposed to go to help out the store but the owner didn't feel well, so I asked Dean to come over. Sometime around 8pm he decided he was tired and wanted to stay home to take care of Duke (the dog) and his Mom. He's still trying to come up with the money. I still haven't offered. I'll see what next week brings. Tomorrow I have to work, run to Clifton park and then catch my flight to Charlotte. I'm excited for a change of scenery. I'm still holding out hope that I cannot drink. Today is 11 days! I can't believe I have come this far. It really has helped keep my emotions in check. I need that right now – especially with Dean around. I also packed some workout clothes and a bathing suit. I'd like to be able to get some exercise in. they have a lap pool. What will be interesting is when Tammy sees my new "additions". Not that they are new – but she doesn't know I did it. I'm going to have to get around the money issue somehow. I mean, she gives me money often for holidays and birthdays. I don't want her to think I blew it on boobs. Which I kind of did. I hope I win big this trip. That would be amazing. It would certainly help. Not just me, but maybe Dean too. He probably forgot I was going now that I think about it, I have told him a few times I was going there. Whether he forgot because of drugs or because he just doesn't really care about me, either way it sucks. I know there is a good person in there just dying to get out. I hate drugs! I hate that he loves them, I hate that he doesn't really know any other life. I hate that he was raised to settle for less than he can be. I hate that he is surrounded by enablers. I hate that I love him. What is it that I love about him? I love his personality and how he makes me laugh. I love that he would be there for me in an emergency if I needed him. I love that he opens my door. I love that he does thoughtful things for me when he is clean. I love his laid- back, adventurous spirit. I love the way my head fits into his shoulder. I love that we can talk for hours and never run out of things to say. I love that we can be classy, gorgeous, sophisticated track-goers. Or wear PJ's and eat pizza on a rainy Sunday. I love that we both love photography. I love that the healthy versions of ourselves is amazing and so compatible too. I love how he makes me feel when I am stressed or scared. I love that he compliments me every day and makes me feel like an amazing, beautiful, capable person. I love that deep down inside, there's a huge, amazing heart. I love to think of having a baby with him. And building a home with him, and being perfectly happy together. I love the amazing, sweet, sober Dean. And I love us together. I just pray I find that guy again – or rather that he finds himself.

Why is it that I can so easily rattle off things that I love about him and not about myself? I'm going to work on me. Because right now, I need to see those loving attributes about myself.

I just finished a book last night "Dirty Rush". Two books down, 28 to go. 226 days in which to do it.

4/1/15

Well I haven't held up much of my commitment to my list the last few days, bit it was worth it for the most part. I went to NC last weekend. Despite being delayed and only going for just over 24 hours, the trip was great. Tammy and Brian won a lot of money and shared with me – as I was getting two massages. I had a good time with Brian, catching up on details of the night, much of what I didn't remember. I drank too much. But luckily, I feel asleep before I made too much of an ass of myself. So now I am back to day 3 of sobriety. But the thing is, it doesn't feel like starting over. I don't even think about drinking when I get home. It is like I broke the habit. I'm not even sure how I drank so much – caught up in the moment I guess. But I think because it didn't happen here, it was easy to not continue. Despite the fact that I won a lot of money, I didn't end up helping Dean get his truck back. He asked his Aunt, and she helped. I did help him with his cell phone -$250, but that is nothing compared to the $1000 he got from her. He has to pay her back, they are family. He could never pay me back and just walk away. Besides I feel like it isn't fair that he should get to spend all his money having fun while I work so hard for mine. I deserve to have fun with mine. He will never be in a position to help me. Add to that the fact that the reason I'm so broke is because of him. My friend Claire found out from a Mom that I was fired from working at school because - according to her – my boyfriend's friends kid told people at school that he was selling drugs. And that while I am innocent – I'm guilty by association. The comment doesn't make sense, obviously. But it loosely connects to Dean's friends girlfriend perhaps talking about it in front of her son, who then reported it at school. Again, why am I still speaking to him. It's so weird. Like I don't need to see him, I just need to know I have him as an option. But I am spending the next week and a half at my aunt's house, dog-sitting, so he can't come there. That is probably a good thing.

I went to Orange Theory fitness with Sally yesterday. It was a good workout. It's nice to try new things. Although I took too much pre-workout and ended up wide awake until 1am, when I finally took some

Benadryl. But at least I overcame my anxiety over trying something new and unfamiliar. Hopefully I can go to the gym while I'm staying in CP this weekend/week.

Sunday is Easter and parents and I are going to Prime for brunch. My step-mother invited me out at 3pm, but after the Christmas nonsense, I declined. I'll stay with Mom all day – she will like that. Maybe staying up there will help me break some other habits too – since the neighbors see everything.

I have some things to check off my list too. I will finish another book tonight. And I have a few good deeds to add as well. I'm not sure about changing a life in a huge way, but that apparently will present itself – I'm sure of it. And I will just "know". I just flipped through these pages and I am impressed with myself – how I am already empowering and living more for me. I am writing and reading so much. Which will bring me closer to my goal of publishing something. I know they are baby steps but it is a long way from where I started. I am stronger that I give myself credit for.

4/7/15 (written in green)

Damit, I didn't mean to grab a green pen – now I'm stuck with it because I'm staying at my aunt's house for 10 days. I guess all this writing needed something to break it up. Dean came over yesterday. It was Easter and he came over around 6pm, probably the earliest he has ever gotten there. Which he owed me since he blew me off on Saturday. But even if he didn't deserve it, I hid Easter eggs with lottery tickets and notes to find tips for a bigger lottery ticket. I loved watching him – I love making him happy. Then we shaved his ridiculous 5+ month beard. I drank too much wine and don't really remember all of it, but we woke up together. It is probably good that I am here for a week – I don't expect him to come back here. So perhaps his heart will grow fonder of me. I don't know I'm sure if that is even possible. I know we could be together. But I also know that I would be accepting the possibility of him relapsing. I also know he will never be on time and will always lie. I know I will live everyday worried that he is manipulating me or hiding something. God, I can't believe any part of me even wants him at all. But he just makes me so happy when he is with me. There is no one who makes me feel how he does. I just love him so. Maybe someday I will meet someone who makes me feel this way, but maybe minus the drama/stress/worries. All I know is that I'm just going to do what makes me happy and live for today, instead of obsessing over the future. Because that hasn't led to anything good in the past. Happy people attract happiness. And as long as things stay ok with Dean, I am a happy person

Speaking of happiness, I'm going back on anti-depressants. Maybe I can stop drinking, for longer than 12 days. Today is day 1. Again. Friday is Sally's birthday. Well actually Thursday is but we are going out Friday. And I don't really want to but I will for her and I will enjoy it. I am going to try to go for a run tomorrow if its nice out. It's time to start working on that 10K. And back on track with the weight loss. I kind of wish I had a beach vacation planned. I need that motivation. I need Dean to want to work out with me. Now that would get me to the gym. How pathetic is that?

4/23/15

It's been so long since I wrote. Not because I couldn't – because I chose not to. I allowed Dean back in – seeing him once a week – alright just for an hour or so before bed. And along with that came slipping into my own old habits associated with my time with him. He could have brought me with him to his sister's wedding if he wanted to. But he didn't. I'm fairly certain it had something to do with his desire to get high without having to hide to hide it from me. Then he canceled our plans two days in a row, and I finally just had it with him. Again. I told him that. He said he was sorry for making me wait around for him. I said I wanted an apology for the way he treated me. I never heard from him. I asked for the keys to the lawn mower and even threatened to call the police (the mower was in my name). Still nothing. It has been over 48 hours. I'm so mad at him. I hate him. How can you treat someone like this? After everything we have been through. After everything he has put me through. I can only assume it is the drugs sucking out any remaining sign of humanity he has left. I so much want the mover and trailer so I can sell it. But I also can't imagine actually calling the police on him. I'm mad but not that mad. I don't think I am physically capable of inflicting that kind of pain on another person. He could go to jail. And then how would I feel? Probably a lot worse than I do now. And would I get dragged into his other problems? I don't want to be associated with him anymore. I don't want to go to jail for being an accomplice or being guilty by association. I'd never survive that. I feel like every day I am fighting to survive. I'm on anti-depressants and I'm so tired. I want to stop them, but part of me wonders if this new-found strength and willingness to step away is because of them. I just don't know anymore.

But today is day 2 of no drinking … Again. I can't drink. I can't stop once I start - I went to work hungover twice this week. That's awful, I got to get my shit straight.

4/30/15

Sorry I have not written in a while. What a week it has been. I heard that Dean was with some of his friends when one of them overdosed and ended up in Albany

Medical Hospital. The police got involved and they were all ticketed and charged with possession of heroin. He should count his blessings that he didn't have more on him and they charge him with dealing. I'm not sure what this means for him, his job, his apartment, his dog. I'm just glad I'm not involved and I wasn't anywhere near him.

Today is day 7 without drinking. I'm finally feeling good about myself. I walked away from Dean and let him go. Without Dean compromising my every thought and plan, I am focused on me and it feels good. I feel blessed with my family and friends. I feel blessed that I have a great future ahead of me and the opportunity to find that someone to share it with. I feel blessed that I am smart enough to stay away from the drugs, the smoking, and bad attitude.

I am going to meet my dreams; my drive is stronger than ever. I am young, I am honest, and I am here to live life!

I don't think I need to journal any more … I'm going to focus on writing my first book! Wish me luck …

P.S. I got the lawn mower and trailer back – I found a buyer on Craigslist, broke even! Amen.

Life Experience

I never knew too much about disabilities until I started teaching or learning how to teach. Then, I had to learn. I realized that it was not all as scary as I thought and that people with disabilities can be really good at the other things and just be generally good people.

10/10/08

I'm not very good at letting things go. I fact, I'm probably the most sentimental person in my family. Not only sentimental but empathetic too. Ted Bear has feelings too. He knows when he is not being treated like the rest of the family. This has become a problem. Once, when I was taller than the bed but shorter than the dresser, I was trying to pack for one of my mother's random road trips we were about to embark on. Her instructions were clear – 2 pants, 2 shirts, socks and underwear and one bear. Not two, not Ted Bear and Fluffy. Only one. One really is the loneliest number. One bear would be left in the cold, dark, lifeless apartment. And one would be forced to sit with me – alone – in the back of the car for hours missing the one that was left alone. How to decide? Certainly, the one I chose would feel special and have a great time while the one alone would be exactly that – alone. Scared, bored, alone, traumatized. I couldn't do it. I tried. I tried really hard. I sat them down and explained this idea of one, that my mother thought would make things easier. But, much as I didn't understand – neither did they. If bears could cry, we would be floating on a bed of tears. Only one solution, take them both. It was the only way. In a fit of internal agony, we went to talk to mom. My mother wouldn't understand- this I knew. Two bears would take up too much room…. or something. She would say no to both of the bears coming with me. Certainly, she couldn't say "no" to their faces. We held hands, and approached the bedroom door. We hesitated and then entered. "Mom" I said in a somber, sullen, yet distressed tone, "I can't choose. I don't want to hurt their feelings."

"HUH?" Mom said, half bewildered, half not paying attention.

"I can't choose," I began. "if I bring one, the other one will be sad but if I don't bring any, I will be the one who is sad. You know the song "One is the loneliest number… "I was babbling. It didn't matter, she wasn't listening. Or was she? "Just bring them both. Are you done packing yet?" What?! Had she really said what I thought she said? Was it true? Could it be? She understood? I didn't give her a chance to take it back. I was off – friends in hand, whistling, myself to happiness. Now my vacation could begin.

*****

"Getting Gizmo"

The first time I saw a picture of a Yorkshire terrier, I was hooked. I am not necessarily a "dog" person but u knew I had to have a yorkie. Little dogs were not yet a trend so I knew it would be difficult to find one locally. I started searching online but most yorkies were between $800-$1000 and I would not be able to see it in person before sending money. And that is a lot of money. So, I had all but given up on the idea. Until one Thursday night in Stewarts. I picked up a Want-Ad digest and turned to the puppy section. And believe it or not, there was a breeder with yorkie puppies. And they even had some with baby doll faces – exactly what I wanted. I called the number immediately. The man said, yes, he did still have 2 puppies but they probably would not be there much longer. Feeling the need for instant gratification, I asked if I could come that night. I knew it was a lot to ask, as it was getting late and it meant he would have to stay at work but he agreed.

When I got to the door of this old Victoria mansion, I was a little nervous. This didn't look like any pet shop I had ever been to. But when the man answered the door with a brown ball of fur no bigger than his palm, I was in love. He handed me the little fur ball and took my cash. I couldn't be happier – even if he did pee on my lap and nip at my fingers all the way home. This little guy would grow up to be not only my dog, but my best friend.

09/19/12

Christmas Day

Christmas is my favorite time of year. When school gets out, the last day before break, I feel like running out the front door, diving into the nearest pile of snow and squishing my arms with wide wing motions. I feel like I am floating high above the earth because I am so excited!

But the fun really begins on Christmas Eve. My grandmother used to make a turkey ball with stuffing and six layer taco dip with cold lettuce, tomatoes and cheese. I would arrive early. The food was so hot it could melt ice and eggnog so cold, I felt like I was in the snow banks outside!

And this was only the beginning.

After grandmas, my father brought me home where I would always get a cup of tea before snuggling up with Mom to watch "a Charlie Brown Christmas." One year, I fell asleep before it came on. So mom woke me up so I wouldn't miss out!

After a long night of eating, smiling, and a cup of tea, I was ready for bed and ready for a morning of presents and fun. Mom would tuck me in tight, kiss me on the cheek and warned me that if I got up too early, there would be no presents for me. I always believed her. But as the years went on, the roles reversed a little. All of a sudden, I started sleeping later and she would be the one who couldn't wait to get up! Instead, she would go downstairs, make me coffee, and tell Gizmo (my puppy) to come up and get me. He would put his little feet on the side of my bed and wine until I picked him up. Then he would like my face until I pulled my sheets back and got up. Then he would run out in the hall and wait like he had to show me the way to the living room!

When I made my way to the bottom of the stairs, my mom would be waiting for me to dive into our presents and Gizmo would be waiting to see what he got.

After presents, we always make a great big breakfast – usually quiche, fruit, home fries, and muffins. When we are done, we get ready and move on to the next house. Here, my aunts, uncles, and cousins come together for the loudest part of Christmas.

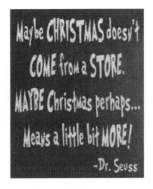

Maybe CHRISTMAS doesn't COME from a STORE. MAYBE Christmas perhaps... Means a little bit MORE!
-Dr. Seuss

09/20/12

<u>Gizmo's Christmas Kisses</u>

 Sometimes I think Gizmo likes Christmas more than I do. When I was little, I used to be the first one to get up Christmas morning. Now Gizmo is always up before me. And he has very little patience. When the light begins to trickle over the horizon and into my room, I know Gizmo won't be far behind.

 Since I don't live with my mom, I go to her house Christmas Eve to wake up Christmas morning. And when I stay at her house, I sleep on the futon in my old room. This means I am lower to the ground than a normal bed, but I am still too far off the ground for my little Yorkie. Since he can't jump high enough to reach me (either he can't or he is too lazy to try) he puts his little paws right up next to my head on the side of the bed and whimpers. And I wake up. But I lay perfectly still with my eyes closed and hope he goes away. But he never does. He just gets louder and louder, and louder. Until I give in, reach over the side, and put him in the bed with me. What he wants is perfectly clear. Exactly one minute of petting and my eyes open. Then I get 7 wet puppy kisses – or enough to get me out of the warmth of my bed. And gizmo gets to open his presents. Yes, he is my dog. And yes, he likes presents too.

3/10/15

Drastic Exaggeration - Hook

Last night, I caught my apartment on fire. Huge flames burst out of my oven and smoke billowed out behind it. I'm lucky I made it out alive!

OK, maybe that isn't exactly what happened, the smoke part is true. But it's not my fault. It was 7:50pm when I put my clay into the oven, but then the bachelor came on. It was the season finale. And it was very dramatic. See, there was this one girl that he really liked, but she wasn't as into him. She wasn't even sure she would marry him. And the other girl, who I actually liked a lot more, she absolutely adored him. I told him that. But, clearly, she was the safe option. The other girl was risky. But I think that's part of what he likes so much about her. It's like that quote "you always want what you can't have" or "The grass is always greener on the other side" Or something like that. Regardless, I bet you already forgot I had clay in the oven, didn't you? See, it wasn't my fault.

Although, I probably shouldn't have turned the oven that high. Actually, I'm not sure how high it was, I kind of just turned the knob and threw the tray in. Did you know that when you overcook clay, it starts bubbling? Weird.

So, all-in-all, it wasn't a total disaster. My apartment had filled with smoke, and I did have to sleep with my sliding glass door open. But it could be worse, right?

Maybe I'll stick to painting.

■ ■

3/12/15

Cell phones weren't meant to swim. And they certainly weren't meant to take the polar bear plunge. And whatever happened to Karma? Aren't good deeds meant to be rewarded? Where is my reward? All I got was a frozen iPhone which now served better as a hockey puck than a communication device.

But the poor lady was stuck. For some reason, she thought trying to drive her 2-wheel-drive Honda up an ice-covered hill, in the middle of the snowstorm was a good idea. Then, she further demonstrated her brilliance by spinning her tires at full speed – because apparently that would conjure up the winter fairies to come and push her out. Like some miraculous act would occur and her car would be levitated out of her self-made ditch.

How could I possibly deny her of my help, especially when I was suitably dressed in knee-high Sorrels and ski gloves. She just looked so pathetic, sitting there behind the wheel of her car, clearly unsure of how to proceed. Amateur.

10/11/12

"My Place to Get Away"

My place to get away, as silly as it sounds, is in my room, on my bed. I have a tall, strong headboard that I lean my pillows against. Then, I can sit up and think, or read, or daydream. But usually, this is where I write. I like to write in my notebook. Sometimes I put the TV on, but sometimes I sit in silence and let all the day's craziness wash away, drift out the window, or pour into my words – captured in the notebook.

"New Friends"

More often than not, middle school can be really tough. When I went to sixth grade, I was out on a team without any of my friends. It was really hard to feel like everyone else had a ton of friends and I didn't. So, when I heard the story of Hannah, I was touched. There was a seventh-grade girl who felt she had no friends. She didn't have anyone to hang out with and no one to eat lunch with. This made her so uncomfortable that she began hiding in a stall in the girl's bathroom for her lunch period. Another 7th grader, Hannah, noticed how much of a hard time this girl was having and she decided to do something about it. She decided to talk to her during gym. After doing this a few times, Hannah asked her to sit with her friends at lunch. She knew her friends might not be happy about this and might make fun of her. But much to her amazement, they didn't. In fact, they were really nice to their new friend and even started reaching out to other kids in similar situations. What if

146

the whole world was as touched as I was? If one person did something like this every day, how much better would the world be?

"Fierce Wonderings"

Growing up, I used to tell people I was an only child. People usually thought it was cool because it isn't that common to not have any siblings. But then as I got older, I started wondering what it would be like to have a sibling. Would it be a girl or a boy? Which would I prefer? If it was a girl, could we share clothes? Would I be mad if she borrowed mine? Or if it was a boy, would he be cool? Or annoying? Now that I am older, would we be friends and hang out? What would it be like to have a lot of sisters and brothers? Would I still have been spoiled? Would I be better at sharing? I don't think I would like it. I think I'm happy as an only child.

1/2/13

"Gizmo the Snoop!"

What was I thinking when I left Gizmo alone, with wrapped presents? I never thought in a million

147

years I would have to worry about him snooping in my gifts. But sure enough, when I came home Christmas Eve, there were my presents, fully unwrapped – shredded paper everywhere! I couldn't believe it! It looked like Christmas morning, after we tear though our presents, except it wasn't morning yet. Because I knew I didn't have the time, or desire, to rewrap everything, I just decided to salvage whatever gifts I could – the rest went under the tree as is. Upon talking to my mom later, I learned Gizmo was looking for a place to bury his bone, and decided a bag of presents was the perfect spot. And in his digging frenzy, destroyed the paper. But how could I be mad at that face.

*****

While the Gastenquays had a strange name, and even stranger ways of doing things, once in a while the father would come through for them and do something cool. One of these times, he decided his 3 kids needed a half pipe in the backyard. And in one short weekend, he had the entire structure together and ready to be used. This was very exciting for all of us. We were tired of rolling up and down slanted driveways on our rollerblades and skateboards. We needed a challenge! We needed to perfect our professional skating skills! The problem was, we weren't professionals. And we were slightly lacking in the "skills" department.

Being a girl, slightly more rational than my male counterparts, I recognized the danger of rolling down a sharp incline on wheels so I took my time preparing for my maiden voyage down the pipe. But alas, the day had come. We had several minutes before our bus came and nothing in the way of entertainment. So I grabbed a board, crawled to the top and listened to my neighbors instructions of how to properly "drop in".

"I got this" I thought. But as I pushed my weight forward over the edge and felt the board slip out from beneath my Nike's, I knew this wouldn't end well. And with a thud on my back, I landed hard and slid to the bottom of the half-circle.

I felt the air leave my body immediately. It was as if a vacuum hose was attached to my esophagus. And as I lay gasping for air, I couldn't help wondering why there were stars out at this hour.

Then I heard it – the familiar grumble of the bus as it rolled down the hill toward our houses. Could I make it? Could I gather enough air to make it to the bus? I knew if my mother had to come all the way home from work because I had done something dumb it would not be pretty.

I propped myself up on my elbows and fought against the constrictions in my chest. I could make it if I had to. And somehow, I did. I am not sure how, as I believe a mild concussion was probably to blame for my foggy recollection. But I made it to school that day, and never again considered skating as a future career endeavor.

It's Not You

If you have never been diagnosed with an anxiety disorder or if you have never experienced anxiety on a level that it could and should be diagnosed, then it is literally impossible to explain how it feels. Because, even the most eloquent, well-versed linguist, with a vocabulary of a scholar, would never be able to articulate a feeling as intense, or as overwhelming as anxiety. Stomach knotting, bone splinting, head-spinning anxiety. I don't mean nervousness like when you are preparing for a test, or about to speak in public and you begin to worry about a temporary slip up of thought. I don't mean the excited butterfly cliché. I mean, straight-up, one step away from fainting anxiety. I mean chronic, lasting, life altering terror. If you still can't imagine the severity, or understand the distinction that only reaffirms my earlier statement. Words do it no justice.

Try for a moment to picture yourself in this situation, you are a new employee, hired at a strange time in the year, brought in to cover someone who left unexpectedly in the middle of a project. Confident in your abilities, and having been hired in a similar fashion before, your day-to-day work is relatively flawless. But one day, you are asked to attend a day full of meetings in various rooms, scattered around your building. Easy enough. So, what would you be concerned about? Nothing? Being prepared? Having a friendly face to site beside? Here is how my mind goes. Where are these rooms? I'll just go tour the building on a break and find them so called rooms, now people will see me and think I'm lost. Someone will offer to help me. People will snicker and whisper to one another, trying to figure out who I am. Maybe I'll stay late one day and do it. But what about the janitors? They probably won't ask or judge me, they are pretty quiet. Okay, mental note. Looking for the rooms - the 600's are here, the 100's are there. Red walls mean 200's. Wait, why are the 300's here. And here is 101, but where is 102? Okay, I'm going to have to ask someone about that. Ugh, where is 959? Here are the 100's, here are the 200's, I thought I found the 400's, where are the 300's? No, I don't know where I'm going. Why is everyone going the other way? Turn and follow. Crap they are going right there to 421. Turn around. Walk like you know where you are going. Straight to your office. I'm already late, 5 minutes late. Maybe I just won't go and if someone asks I'll just say I couldn't find it. I have to pee. Leave office, enter restroom. And that's when it happens. The tears well up in your eyes. Why won't anyone help me. This isn't fair. I have to be there, there will be an empty seat. This will look awful. Dammit, don't cry your makeup will smear. You are already 10 minutes late. People are already going to stare. Oh my God, think of something funny while you wash your hands. You haven't looked in the downstairs front wing yet, try that. Or ask someone! Who? Everyone is in the meetings. Oh! Thank God, a friendly, non-threatening face.

Are you lost? Yes, dear copy lady I am? Please help you angel of God, please. And all of this accompanied by a heartbeat increased almost twofold, palms immediately drenched in sweat and a slight trembling of the hands. Add to a pit in the stomach, a highway express of irrational fear, and welcome to my life. And that's mild. And a fairly regular occurrence. No, I can't control it. Yes, the rational part of my brain knows I don't need a fight or flight response at this very second. No, that makes no difference. So, if you ask me if I want to meet you somewhere "new" and I say no, it is not you. I know you. And if you want me to attend a party and I say no, its not you, I know you. I

153

can talk to you. I can be around you without my heart racing or stumbling over my words. But the other people I don't know, I can't. It just isn't worth it. These "new" experiences simply are not worth the excruciating, debilitating anxiety I would need to overcome. And I'm sorry for that.

Now, if you stay with me, next to me and promise not to leave my side for so much as a second, I'll do whatever you want – and I might even enjoy it. If you promise to get lost with me, make conversation with the people around us, and never leave me vulnerable or alone, then I also would not be able to explain what anxiety feels like, because you ease that from me entirely. Yes, I know this sounds crazy – makes me sound like I have some kind of dependency issue ... I probably do. But this is me and I can't help it.

So next time you are irritated because I won't go somewhere and I say no, it's not you ... I know you.

▪▪▪

The dorm halls of Oneonta State University were much different than those of my small private Catholic college in upper-class Loudonville, New York. These halls were smaller, longer, darker. Doors were shut at nine a.m. as the dwellers inside the caves were busy recovering from the alcohol-induced festivities of the night before. As I slide my back down the cold painted cinderblock wall and landed on the similarly donned floor, I immediately became aware of how this would not be the birthday I had hoped for. In fact, it would be the third worst day of my life.

*****

In upstate New York, fall brings with it a rainbow of autumn and gold splashed with cherry red apples and topaz pumpkins. The temperature plummets from the warm August humidity to a crisp fall dampness. The sun sets shorter a little earlier and rests a little later as the days freeze into winter.

That day was a true Autumn day. The sun warmed as the breeze sent chills up my arms. The windows surrounding two sides of my airy college classroom were wide open. Apparently, I was the only warm-blooded person in the room. The cars on the city street beneath us were drowned out by the sound of my professor. She was an awkward woman. Young, short, plump and not particularly attractive. That's not to say she was unattractive, but more like one of those little dogs with the smushed face. They are so ugly that you feel bad for them and suddenly they are adorable.

The class was on Native American Literature, yet somehow, I'm sure I now couldn't disseminate a Native American epic from a Junie B. Jones book. In fact, the only thing that kept me from falling off my cushioned chair to the cold cement beneath me was analyzing the professor. She had come in the last class and began to lecture when for no apparent reason she chocked. Oh what? Her tongue? Her spit? Who knows. But no one moved. Even when she requests that someone turn over their water to her, no one moved. We all just stared in pure astonishment. What kind of person would want to drink out of another's water bottle? Let alone a professor. How does she know what germs are in there? Well, she didn't care. Reaching for the closest water bottle to her, she snatched it, sipped out of it, placed it on her desk and promised the mortified student it would be replaced. And on she went with the lecture. Now how does one forget that. Perhaps if she had not chocked I could focus on the course content rather than trying to analyze my pug-faced professor.

Sometime between my daydreaming of choking professors and shivers from the damp cool air billowing through the windows, I had found time to draw hearts marked by M&E and sign the name I dreamt of bearing … Erica Hayner, Mrs. Matthew Hayner, Erica Ladu-Hayner. Yeah, I was pathetic. Twenty years old, drawing hearts across my notes. But I was so in love with my man fighting the war in Afghanistan. Gone eight months… not heard from in two weeks. I may have been beyond in love. Perhaps it was more of an obsession. It is true, distance makes the heart grow fonder. I was proof.

Anyway, staring out the window, deciding whether the gray puffy clouds bearded a storm or were just a tease, I heard the heavy wooden door push open. Glancing to see who was disrupting our humble abode, I chocked. On my tongue? On my spit? Who knows. I also don't know how long I sat motionless or how I prevented myself from fainting. Standing in the doorway fully covered in camouflage, beanie cap in hand, stood my love, my obsession. Springing to my feet, virtually flying to the door, I flung my arms around his neck, sinking my face into his warm shoulders and soaking his collar with tears. How did he know where I was? When had he gotten back? How long was he home for? I didn't know but I didn't care. Gasping for breath between sabs of glee, Matt pried me off of him, grabbed my books and led me out of the room. What the pug-faced Native American lit expert and all of her little Indians were thinking was beyond me. My sweetheart was home!

Well okay, he was gone for eight months and I hadn't heard from him in two weeks. Only when he got back from Afghanistan, he wasn't in digi's, he was in a hospital gown. And he didn't whisk me away from my classroom, I drove six hours at midnight to his hospital room. And he wasn't my huge, strong Marine he had left as. He was smaller and shorter and sick. Very, very sick.

Hearts Lust

The infinite possibilities induced by the heart's lust for the unattainable return of devotion are too vast and intense that to try to explain or to express it would be futile. There is no way for me to recount the intangible force which compelled me, no, allowed me to do all that I did. To make it out alive. To not only live, function, succeed. But to thrive and grow while all the world around me appeared, to all whom watched from the side, to disintegrate, to deteriorate, to die, piece by piece until all that was left was me. Standing. Alone. Sad and so very alone. And yet still be standing. Strong and square-shouldered in the face of gale winds as they threatened to tear away at me, tatter my being, force me to topple. But it is that lustrous desire which held me erect, unshaken.

I will never be sure what woke me. I will choose to believe that we had become so solidly joined, connected at the heart that I did in fact share his body's circadian rhythm, my body reacting in the exact same way that his did. Or perhaps he woke me, deathly afraid of death, or peacefully accepting it. I did not awake with a jolt, but not in a sleepily confused kind of way. But I awoke as if I had never been sleeping. Glided out of the bed, placing my socked feet onto the cool tile floor. My actions had by now become so routine, so habitual that I mindlessly dampened a cloth and eased onto the sliver of bed next to Matt, my left foot stabilizing my body. But as I sat to clean his face, suck the liquid from his throat with the apparatus stationed beside his head, I was filled with a numbness and knew it was not the time to be housekeeping. As his eyes met mine, there was a kind of exchange. A silent stillness transmitted all the words that we had held so near and dear, the childlike nicknames, the silent gestures, the words and I love you's that would never sound the same. Everything that needed to be said was said, though I repeated them aloud. I love you, I'll always love you. I rubbed his cheek with my thumb and set my hand on his heart, trying to memorize the sound, the feel. And as he looked over my shoulder at some invisible peace, I heard the last breath, a kind of choke or gargle. It might be possible that time stood still at that moment. The world ceasing to exist so that I might process and live. So that Matt might leave in a wrinkle of time. There was nothing outside of us. We stood in a great silent abyss, a black hole is which nothing exists, but us.

Death is one of those things that is so difficult to believe as it can never be seen, heard, tasted, smelled, or touched. Death isn't one thing but rather a lack of things. Completely intangible, it is merely a concept proven only by its results and our senses' reactions to those results. We hear the sobs of those crying over the feelings of abandonment. We taste the tears that burn our cheeks and cringe from the scent of musty funeral parlors. These are the things that live in us and prove death to be real. But in that moment, I had no senses. I had no proof. So, as I lay my head to his chest, searching for some evidence of life, I was left with an absence. Enough absence to prove that this idea, this concept of death had actually materialized. I was not sure of the appropriate measures. Opening the heavy wooden door and announcing to the hallway and all listening that I had a dead corpse on my hands did not seem appropriate. Pressing the nurse call button and waiting ten minutes for someone to stroll in, expecting a nuisance request did not seem fair. And yet, leaving this body seemed taboo. But God had thought of all this. And as I pulled on the heavy door, there was a nurse standing at the adjacent station. Simply waiting for a purpose, it seemed. "Umm, can you help me?" was all I could think of. Perhaps I should have warned her. Perhaps I should have explained, but it didn't seem necessary. She knew. It was written on my face and his. I returned to my sliver of bed and stared as she reached around me to hear for a heartbeat then tried unsuccessfully to close his cold eyelids. They wouldn't stay shut. I stared at the bottom of his lids where the blood would normally pulse, causing a deep pink to exist and wondered how long it took for a body to turn cold. Wondered what it was that paced through his mind as he looked at me for the last time. Wondered what it was he saw over my shoulder, or who it was that had come for him.

A flurry began around me, I think. But I remained on my sliver. Oblivious to it all, not trying to ignore it but succeeding anyway. It was as if I had just kicked a giant hornet's nest, causing a stir of madness and yet none of the bees bothered with me, or chose to sting me, or perhaps they did but the numbness remained so strong I didn't feel it. I didn't feel it until I caught sight of the velvet maroon case atop a folding metal stretcher. So narrow, so shallow, a human could not possibly fit inside. It seemed so morbid, so dead. But as I watched the round man wheel it closer and closer to the door of the room I had come to know as my home, I felt my legs giving way beneath me and my clothes catching on fragments of limestone as I slid down the cold hospital wall. My eyes burned from my temples as the incinerating tears approached the whites of my eyes.

The Last of Matt

The one orange chair in the first row, situated amongst the other yellow chairs, I was told was where I was to sit. This is how they know who to hand the flag to. This is how they distinguish "next of kin" among a sea of tear-encrusted faces. This is how they know where to kneel as they lay the triangular created symbol of American pride as they recite their heart-felt sorry for "your loss".

So there I sat. Singled out again. The only one in an orange chair. The only one worthy of owning a flag. The only one addressed in the recitation. The only one who was actually part of any piece of the last six months of his life.

It was the middle of July and the clear skies allowed for the high moon sun to bake the air. But somehow, dressed in my black sweater, black pants, and black heels, I felt nothing. I wasn't hot, I wasn't cold. I wasn't sad, I didn't want to cry. I wanted to be an absentee. I wanted to not be present for this spectacle. I was numb. I sat in a dead gaze at the red rose collage donned with a ribbon reading "Nuff". I wondered how many people had tried to figure that out. How many people actually knew what it meant. And how many people hadn't even noticed. Absorbed in their own self-pity, guilt and drama scenes, hadn't even focused their attention to the coffin.

The click-click of the rifles pinning caught my attention as the first seven shots sang out, filling the blank space between stone white crosses and stars of David. My whole body shuttered to the blast slamming on my ear drums. It couldn't get worse. No other moment of my life could hurt more that this particular second. No other moment could ever leave me so hollow – so alone.

*****

It was not planned, my attending Oktoberfest. Or any of the ensuing events. A long weekend was not worth the time it was going to take to get to Munich and the price of the international ticket. But when Mom offered to pick up the tab as a graduation present, I knew it would be silly to refuse. And so I packed up a small suitcase of jeans, tees, and Adidas and headed to the airport for a long, lonely, 2 leg trip to Germany where Mom and Ed were already. Albany to LaGuardia on the puddle jumper was easy, basic, jump as good as could be expected. It wasn't until I arrived at the gate for the Munich flight that the events began to unfold in no typical, basic, or easy manner. As I sat against the cold glass shielding passengers form their awaiting jets, I glanced around and noticed that this particular flight appeared to be filled with one standard profile set of people. Mid-twenties, early thirties, adventuresome, happy, and ready to party in Munich. Oktoberfest. Low and behold, I was not alone. So when the voice came across the localized public address system announcing a 2 hour delay of our flight, I was also not alone in my feelings of distress, disappointment, and general irritation. Though I did not express my frustrations quite as vocally as my fellow travelers for most of them had 2-3 friends with whom they could commiserate. I was alone. Not lonely, just alone. However, I must have appeared lonely as one of the few atypical passengers of this late flight took up residence beside me. "Going to Munich?"

"Trying." I shrugged. This mid-forties reincarnate of a left over 80's thug rubbed me the wrong way. Not literally, not yet anyway. But he was a little out-of-place and that made me nervous. Why do I always attract the child molester look-alikes and the midlife-crisis victims. Just once I would like a normal, standard, decent looking male to approach me and have a real, normal, decent conversation with me.

"Me too."

I was almost afraid to ask. "For business or pleasure?"

"A little of both, I think." He stared at me. Perhaps awaiting an inquiry into clarification. I wasn't biting. I hate when people do that. Say what you want to say. I stared back. "Headed to Oktoberfest?"

I could have whipped something back at him. Something witty, obnoxious and snobby. Could have congratulated him on his profound assumption. I refrained.   He was trying. "Yeah, I am, meeting some people there." That should be enough to keep the mindless questions at bay temporarily. I considered moving. I considered excusing myself. I was not interested in a new friend. Not this kind. It seemed a little too much like the beginning of some horror movie where the girl gets drugged, abducted, and sold into the Czech sex slave market. I pretended to be checking on the flight status and removed myself before any more prodding into personal life details could occur.

I wandered the airport, shopped and returned to find the board proclaiming another hour had been added to our delay. And the majority of the passengers had relocated to the incandescent lit clue bar adjacent to the gate. I sat and stared and longed. And realized for the first time that I was lonely. I wanted to go into that bar and drink away the hours with fellow commiserates and forget the anger I was now feeling toward the airline and forget the anxiety that perhaps we would be spending the night in this city and forget the disappointment that my already-short trip was now being threatened to be cut to mere hours to be spent in Germany. I wanted a friend too. So much so. I decided, that I was willing to risk a trip to the sex slave market. It didn't take long to spot my bald-headed friend. And it didn't take much effort to solicit an offer of a drink and snack in the bar across the way. And it didn't take much time for me to transform into my alter ego- the one who can strike up conversation with anyone, anywhere, anytime, and really become the center of entertainment and attention. I had made the friends I was seeking, and the situation was starting to look up. As the rounds were passed around, I promised my new friends a ride across the ocean on a privately chartered yacht. I even declared that if someone could get ahold of a boat company, I would personally fund the expedition to ensure we could all attend the festivities we were so looking forward to. I would be the saving grace for all of us. Just keep the drinks coming.

Fortunately for everyone involved, and my bank account, the flight was not canceled. But as they announced, at 10 o'clock pm, that we would in fact take off to Germany, it was apparent that there would be some discrepancy and tension developing soon. We lined up at the gate in no apparent order (most were lucky if they even knew where they were headed at this point) and were forced to speak to at least one flight attendant before proceeding down the jet way. One at a time, we were being discreetly screened for sobriety and ability to remain civilized and seated for the duration of the flight. My California threesome friends approached the warden before me and I watched as one of the fine young, yet drunken, men were given a fair warning and informed that if he could not walk to the end of the jet way in a straight line on his own, the captain would not allow him

169

to board. He was screwed. He couldn't see the jet way, let alone walk down it unassisted. Perhaps in a moment of poor judgment on his friends' behalves, he was left behind. I proceeded, smiled, and managed to slide by unscathed. I did however, test my limits once aboard and having a voluminous verbal dispute with an ex via cell phone. I'm fairly certain I informed him that I hoped the plane would crash so that he would have to live with the guilt of being extremely mean to me in my last few minutes of my life. I am also fairly certain that a passenger several rows behind me was the one who informed me of my unnecessarily high tone and potential for removal from the flight. He was a good new-found friend. I wonder what his name was.

This three-hour pre-gaming for Oktoberfest in LaGuardia Airport allowed me to easily slip into a post take-off beer coma and sleep for the entirety of the flight. As we touched down in the culture-rich Munich, I whipped the drool streak from my chin, fingered combed my hair and prepared for the party of a lifetime.

Oktober in September

I'm not sure if Oktoberfest is something that people outside of Europe really know about. Sounded really "cultural" to me. A little bit of history, a little bit of carb-rich food, maybe some oversized blond men throwing logs or something. But I guess what they don't teach you in school is the true meaning of the holiday. The month. The month that is actually a misnomer to the Holiday. Because the only part of this festival that actually takes place in October is the collection of garbage, lost articles, and other random choochkie that is left behind by the 2 million people who flood the grounds on this yearly occasion. I was acutely unaware of the intense partying that accompanied this lovely festival. Partying isn't even the right word. Because before I attended this ridiculously extravagant event, I had never been to a party where shouting in 38 different languages, communicating with tables mates via hand gestures, marching across the tent on table tops, a toast every 32 seconds or so, snorting white peppermint powder, and drinking from glasses heavier than my head were all commonplace and actually expected. And the hardest part of it all was finding a place to sit. Because unless you arrive at 9am and stand in line to rush the tables like a herd of cattle after a grass feast, it is nearly impossible to seat 3 people together. And without a seat, you cannot be served. And without being served, who the hells wants to deal with the screaming, marching toasting, and snorting? But through some divine power of the gods, we somehow lucked out. My mother forging the way, me close behind her, and her boyfriend strategically hidden behind me, we squeezed, ducked, and prodded our way up and down some 50 aisles looking for a square inch of real estate on one of the picnic benches. Anything would have worked. We would have sat on top of each other if necessary. But it wasn't. A nice group of drunken Irish men were clearly occupying more than the needed amount of space for such small people and graciously moved aside for us. All three of us (much to their dismay – they didn't see the boyfriend) and so the party began. And the beer flowed. And Mom's boyfriend fell off the bench. One down. And some more beer flowed.

I mentioned the incredible amount of language spoken, no, shouted here. But what I failed to mention is the accents that come along with the eclectic mix of party-goers. Our table mates were no exception. I hadn't a freaking clue what any one of those boys were talking about. Apparently, it is very commonplace to add "boy" or "like" to the end or beginning of every single sentence. "What da f*** da ya f***in mean buy? Ya f***in windin me up like." And to add to it, they were drunk and slurring. And I was drunk and 50 IQ points slower. It was a f***in disaster like. But the beer flowed. And flowed. And we sang. And the beer flowed. And we prosted. And the beer flowed. And Mom sent her boyfriend home in a cab. And the beer flowed. And the guy sitting next to me, who had been very quiet and hadn't even glanced in my direction, spoke to me. And the beer flowed. And I used a process of elimination to decipher about a quarter of what he said. And the beer flowed. And we discovered we had the same name- Eric and Erica. And the beer flowed. And he wanted a balloon so I traded a dirty Italian a kiss for the balloon. And the beer flowed. And I fell in drunk-love. And the beer flowed. And I made out with him. And the beer flowed.

There were several things wrong with this situation. All clear to me now:

1. Mom put her shitfaced boyfriend in a cab, paid the driver, and sent him to the hotel with a key so that I could continue to drink. We didn't give him a second thought for the entire evening.

2. I kissed a dirty Italian.

3. I kissed a drunk Irishman.

4. We all snorted a mysterious minty substance.

5. I sent Mom home on a bus, paid the driver, and hoped she made it alive.

6. I left with the Irishman, went to his hostel, and continued to drink rum and diet.

Sounds like the start to any of those Hostel movies out there. But those movies weren't out yet. And the beer flowed. And what happened in that hostel room is between me, Eric.

When I finally made it back to my mother's room, it was light out. And I laid on the edge of the bed, beside my mother and her boyfriend, and couldn't wait for my Irishman to call me. He had my mother's cell number. Of course he would call. Why wouldn't he? Why would he? This phone wasn't leaving my sight all day. And it didn't. And he didn't. And I didn't.

And if I hadn't left my brand new Nicole Miller leather jacket in his room that night. And if I hadn't gone back to his hostel on a drunken mission to retrieve said jacket, and if I hadn't been making such a scene in the lobby trying to get the elevator to work, and if he hadn't been sitting in the bar stool closest to the door in which he could see the lobby, and if we hadn't figured out that I accidentally gave him the wrong country code, and if we hadn't blamed this all on fate and destiny, and if we hadn't allowed this to spark a 9 month international relationship, we wouldn't have gotten married. And I wouldn't be filing for divorce. And my shrink wouldn't be able to afford that summer condo in Vermont that my insurance is surely funding.

I knew it was wrong but I saw no alternative. I knew I would regret it but somehow, it seemed okay at the moment. I'm actually very good at doing things I know I will regret. I just kind of do it real fast and get it over with before my conscience can overtake me. Its like jumping into a 2 ft. deep pool from a twelve-foot cliff. You know it's a bad idea but once you leave that ledge there is nothing anyone can do to stop you. And so you crash and get very hurt. But you did it to yourself. You knew the implications. You just chose to ignore them. For some reason, you thought that the pool would be deeper once you got there and everything would be okay. And that is exactly why the divorce rate is skyrocketing. The pool is as deep, and only as deep as it looks. Trust it. And you better damn well not jump just because several people have assured you it is deep. You see it clearer than they do. They aren't standing on this ledge next to you. They aren't the ones about to jump- and be crushed. I wish someone had given me this advice. Because as Eric's traveler visa ran out and we came to the realization that overstaying his visa would make him an illegal alien forever, there were two options. 1- He could go home, and risk the customs officers refusing his reentry due to the extended amount of time he had already spent here. Or 2- We could get married and apply for his green card with me as his sponsor. And I had 32 hours to decide. I didn't want to marry him. But I was unsure if I was completely done with him yet. And it seemed to me that sending him home and never knowing for sure if he was the one or not would be worse than marrying him. And it wasn't really a wedding that we had to go through- just some simple paperwork at the courthouse. That easy. Bring two witnesses to criminal court in the worst part of town and the judge will sign off that you are not drunk or lacking capacity to make such decision right before she goes in to hear the criminal cases. And poof- you're screwed. Well, married. I laughed. I laughed the whole way to the courthouse. I laughed the whole time we waited for the judge. I laughed as I signed the papers. I laughed as the witnesses signed. I laughed all day. I had to. Because I knew this was the wrong choice. And I knew I had made a mistake. And it was all I could do to keep myself from jumping off the bridge into the Hudson. But hindsight- that would have been a better choice than the headlong dive I took off the cliff into a two-foot pool. That hurt.

And no one knew. Me, Eric, Jordan, Dee. That was it. And that was all that would ever know. Ha. Until

177

now, I suppose. Sorry. Once it was all said and done, I was filled with the worse kind of regret, angst, shame, anger, hatred, sadness, and overall anxiety. There was no part of me that contained an ounce of happiness or peace. I was at war with myself. And there was no one to talk to. NO one. My thought process brought me to the conclusion that this would all be a lot better if there were no secrets involved. Unfortunately, knowing my mother, this was not an option. The next best thing? An engagement. At least if I was engaged- it was kind of like telling everyone the truth. It was close. Eric agreed. Of course he did, he was broke and along for the ride. He bought me a ring. A ring I picked out. And paid for. And picked up. And he proposed. A proposal I planned. And drove us to. And faked. It was all fake. It was a disaster. I'm not sure there was even 2 feet of water in that pool. Pretty sure I jumped into solid concrete.

*****

I had no idea what room he was in. I knew it was in the corner to the right off the elevator. I knew it was on the second or third floor. I knew I would never do this sober. But I also knew there was no stopping me now, drunk, a product of Oktoberfest.

I stood from my barstool, leaving Mom and Ed to watch my things, and headed next door. Pounding on the elevator button, part of me wondered why the drunk Germans in the lobby were laughing. Part of me didn't care, part of me was just trying to stand up straight. Within a few minutes as one of the German's swiped his room key across a pad, finally allowing the doors to open, I caught another door open from the corner of my eye. From the hostel bar emerged what I had been searching for. My leprechaun. My Mr. Eric Moloney.

I was wrong about the floor, it was the fourth. I was wrong about his not calling, I gave the wrong phone number. I was wrong about a lot but searching him out was right.

*****

Eric

     I knelt in my seat, trapped against the window. Why do I always insist on a window seat? I'm forever waiting for an 80 year-old man to collect his unnecessary carry on from the overhead all the while protecting my own head from the inevitable dropping of the suitcase by the fragile man. I sigh, I tap, I fidget, they never get the point, let me out! But especially now, now! I waited 39 days for this moment. All that stood between me and my new love was customs, and a geriatric patient fighting with the overhead.

Finally! Movement! I could feel the rush of cool, clean air sweep up my sweater as I crossed over the jet way. I hoped my luggage followed me, I hoped customs was short. I couldn't wait to see that wide Irish smile, open arms, waiting for me.

As I rushed through customs, my excitement blinding my sensibility, the pending elation was almost overwhelming. I dragged my 55 pound paisley-print suitcase into the sea of awaiting faces. My eyes darted from face to face – too old, too young, too dark, too woman. Where was he? He certainly had arrived. He certainly came to find me. Where could he be. Babe! Please appear, I'm tired, I'm stressed, I'm excited, I need a hug.

Nothing.

People filtered by me into awaiting arms, into awaiting cabs. Their suitcases knocking mine as they scurried past. My heart sunk. Something had happened. He wouldn't leave me here, in London, alone. My phone didn't work, he couldn't call. I'm alone...

There he is!!!

■■■

Teacher-mares (09/23/15)

The first day of school always brings a multitude of emotions. Not just for students, but for teachers as well. One week before school, every single year, for my years that I have been a teacher – the teacher-mares begin.

I'm a teacher and I have nightmares ... teacher-mares. Sometimes they are related to school – sometimes not. Sometimes I dream that I am back in school myself. And it doesn't help that I went to this school too!

This year, I had a dream that I was back in high school. I had to get supplies from my locker, but I couldn't remember my combination. I'm a very conscientious student, so you can imagine this really upset me. When my alarm went off, I woke up thinking that I had to go to school- but as a student. I jumped out of bed and ran to the closet to find clothes – but I found myself knocked to the ground, very confused, and with a very sore hand. Of course I did- I no longer live in my childhood home. And there is a wall where my closet used to be. Laying there on my bedroom floor it accrued to me- I am not in high school. My closest is not on this wall. And it is still august.

Go back to sleep Miss Ladu. Go back to sleep.

*****

We are all living
in cages with the
door wide open.
George Lucas

Polka Dot Persuasion

When I moved into my new house in Latham, I was so excited. I owned my first house ever. I had my very own kitchen, my very own backyard, and my very own mailbox. None of this was particularly interesting – yellow and white kitchen, green yard, and boring black mailbox. Just a simple black metal box on a simple black metal post. Why would anyone want my mailbox? I have no idea, which is why I was so confused when I came out of my house one day only to find that my entire mailbox was gone! Fence post and all! It was just a small black hole in my yard now! My first mailbox, stolen in the dark of night. I wanted to be sad. But I couldn't. Because I was SO mad! This was a crime! A crime against the mailbox owners of the world. I decided I would make sure no one ever considered ever stealing my mailbox ever again. I got in my car, sped to Home Depot, and purchased a new boring black mailbox. But I knew about the mailbox snatchers of America so I bought white paint and concrete – a LOT of concrete. Enough concrete to make sure that the post would never, ever come out of the ground again. And the white paint? I decided to make sure no one ever, EVER considered stealing my mailbox again. After all, who would want a polka dot mailbox? And I was right, it worked! In fact, not only did no one steal my polka dot mailbox, but the mailbox thieves actually returned the original mailbox. They must have felt bad that I had to look at such an ugly one!

*****

OMG Cupcake

I consider myself a cupcake aficionado- I mean, I have had cupcakes from different bakeries, in different states, in different countries. So, when I heard about Coccadott's OMG cupcake – I knew I had to try it! And when I went to a birthday party and she had some, I knew it must be divine intervention – fate wanted me to taste the cupcake to end all cupcakes.

At first glance, one would not necessarily choose this cake over all the other in the sparkling clear case. The bland light camel tan does not look to appealing. But I decided not to judge it before trying it. Pulling the hardened flower from the top, I gently set it aside. I know what these taste like and I didn't want to disrupt the real experience of the OMG cupcake.

I had planned to simply lick some frosting off the top. This is always my favorite part and I figured if this wasn't good, the rest was doomed. But what I experienced was rather shocking. I was unable to remove any frosting as it was coated in a hardened shell. The shell was going to need to be broken and eaten separately. I tapped the top with a fingernail and used the first chuck to scoop up some delicious frosting. And as the buttery sugar approached my mouth, my nose told me this was going to be amazing. And I was right. My tongue curled the decadent excitement and begged for more. I decided to remove the wrapper and bite into the soft brown sponge – even if it meant a nose full of sugar. The bottom was hard as the base was made of Oreo smothered in peanut butter. Frosting hardened over frosting over cake upon a peanut butter coated Oreo…OMG

*****

Wildcat cheer   (10/5/12 – Erica Cheerleading Coach)

"Who are, who are,

Who are we? We are, We are, We are thee, Crestdale Wildcats, The best !!!!"

"Are you ready? Are your ready for this? Do you like it? Do you like this? Shoot Shoot. In the hoop. Shoot, shoot in the hoop!" " Int-imi-dat-ion. Intimidation! Intimidation."

"Get up, get up. Get up out your seat, and get into the Wildcat Beat! " " Hey! You knew the story, so tell the whole wide world, this is wildcat territory!"

*****

An experience that has shaped me (10/25/13)

When I was asked to coach cheerleading, I was psyched! I had just moved to Charlotte, NC and I really didn't know anyone. I wasn't sure how I was going to pass the time after school. Maybe I would just read a lot? It sounded like I was going to be in for a long, boring school year. Little did I know, that wasn't going to be the case at all. And by the end of the year, I would be wishing for a boring, quiet day.

186

Tryouts were intense. Over 60 girls were trying out for the honor to hold Wildcats pom-poms. That meant dozens of girls would be sent home, some even, in tears. But it also meant, I would have an amazing team of 12 girls – the best of the best – to share the season with. But as the days went on, I realized we were sharing more than just a season as coach and athletes, these girls became a second family to me. With 10 hours of practice, 2 games a week, not to mention countless hours on the bus, we ate together, laughed together, and even sometimes cried together. I am not really sure how I would have survived without them. And it taught me a lot. I was a coach and a teacher, but my cheerleaders were coaching and teaching me too.

And it made me realize the value of family and friends. I had a temporary substitute family in Charlotte, but nothing could replace the real thing.

That was my last year in Charlotte. When June rolled around and school came to a close, so did my desire to live far away. I packed up my car and came back to New York, back to family and back to my friends.

*****

<u>Abby</u>

I stood in awe as this girl, no this beast, whom I had once considered a step-sister, burst through the garage entryway, past me in the foyer and stormed up the stairs. She wasn't supposed to be here. Upon visiting her father last, much before I had arrived, she stood in the driveway in the middle of the night drunkenly announcing to the world what a lowlife he was. She had since been banished. But yet here she was. Charging through the house, rescuing her 15-year-old sister from the perils of her God-awful Nanny, me. Rebecca, being an impressionable yet troubled girl with a crazy for a sister and a drunk for a mother, sided with Abbie (her sister). TJ, who I would come to find out never knew about this mission and simply thought he was driving 12 hours to accompany this crazy on a beach vacation, stood in the breezeway in awe and bewilderment.

"If I were you, I would leave." I warned him.

"Uh, I really have to pee." He responded

"So go, and get out or I will call the police." I
said.

The hooves of any angry elephant crazily came
pounding down the carpeted staircase.
"Who do you think you are? Destroying our family,
splitting up our parents? You aren't even his
daughter…" They flew past me, arms full of bedroom
belongings. Remain calm I told myself. Be the bigger
person, I could hear my mother's voice in my
heard. Taking a deep breath, I opened the garage door
behind them to only find an empty driveway and Taco
Bell garbage where the car had been.
They were gone.
And so it began.

■■■

Students and Teachers (10/5/12)

When Lander walked into my classroom for the
first time, she didn't stand out as someone I would
necessarily think of as any different than anyone
else. After all, the first day is always a little crazy and a

little stressful and it takes all of my attention just to be sure everyone gets where they need to be – especially when it is all of our first years in the building. But as weeks pass and I get to know names, and become acquainted with my students, I always find something unique or special about every single one. For Landan, it was her passion for cheerleading. As cheer coach, that gave us a lot to talk about. And we talk. A LOT! She told me when my shoes were pretty and I told her when back tuck needed work. She is currently one student who had an impact on me. Several years ago, I had a student named Ashley. We always joked that she was a "mini-me." She had long blonde hair and dressed a lot like me. She came to see me during lunch and made fun of my mini carrots. She told me when I was too hyper in class and I told her when she produced an amazing piece of writing. There are many students I remember one of my last few years of teaching for one reason or another. Often, I wonder which one's remember me and why? Do they remember me as being their most strict teacher, easiest teacher, smartest teacher? Or am I one of those teachers who just blend into their memories - - never to be thought of again?

I know I have had teachers like that – I can't remember my 2nd grade teacher's name, let alone what she looked like. But my 1st, 2nd and 3rd grade teachers (I moved in the middle of the year) both came back into my life as an adult and have had a profound effect on my life. My 6th grade teacher remains clear as day in my mind too. He was mean, belittling, and sarcastic. He taught me a lot. He taught me exactly what kind of teacher I <u>never</u> want to be. And so, I take a vow to my students. I will never give you a rude comment. I will never respond with a sarcastic tone- unless your question warrants it. I will never give you more than you can handle or push you beyond your capabilities. And if I do, feel free to call me out on it. Because I am here for <u>you</u>.

Passarte Writing (10/5/12)

    As a teacher, there are things that make me really happy. Things that other people – non-teacher people – would think are silly. For me, seeing a passion for writing develop in my students makes me so happy. When I look around the room during writers' workshop and see their pencils moving furiously across the page, and furrowed in deep concentration, I know something special is happening. I know great thoughts are being recorded. I know life stories are being recorded and valuable information documented. And I know at least one person in the room, writing is becoming something they look forward to, rather than something they dreed. Too often, I hear "I hate writing" and that makes me sad. What you really mean is "I have not yet found the kind of writing I enjoy." Therefore, I have made it my personal mission to change that. And the day I hear "can I write more?" is the day I know my mission is accomplished.

*****

I was just being myself. My crazy silly self. The one that comes out only when I'm really happy, or love the people I'm with, or gotten a lot of sleep, or consumed a lot of sugar … or … alcohol. As was the case this night. Amber had had enough of my twirling on the dance floor, demanding more shots with dirty names, and babysitting my purse as I randomly disappeared in the dense crowd of the local college bar. She wanted to leave. Relying on her as my never intoxicated "DD", I followed. Well, I didn't follow completely that easy. I strolled down Pearl Street toward the bottom of Chapel Hill and spun twice in my best ballerina fashion at the bottom of the hill. All the while ignoring Amber's gentle coaxing "Erica, stop your drunk F$%#@g shenanigan's and get up here or I swear to God, I will leave without you!" I stopped twirling and glanced up the hill only to realize how far I had fallen behind. I was …. (unfinished)

*****

Fierce Wonderings – Pencils (09/17/14)

How do so many pencils end up on the floor? I mean, doesn't anyone notice that they are constantly out of pencils? Or that their Crayola box is missing its blue pencil? And where do they all end up? How come, every year I buy 10 more packs of pencils- and all my students buy new packs of pencils?   Where did the old ones go? Is there some giant stockpile of missing pencils somewhere? Do the custodians have a bin of abandoned pencils hiding in the back? Is there a pencils fairy who comes around and takes all of the lonely pencils? Maybe the pencil fairy builds houses out of pencils. Maybe the colored ones are used for doors and shutters. Maybe the house gets bigger and bigger every day. Maybe there are hundreds of pencil fairies out there in pencil houses with pencil shutters and pencil doors.

<u>5 Top Personal Values</u> (10/7/14)

1. Family togetherness

2. Empathy / Compassion

3. Creativity

4. Honesty

5. Health

My #1 top personal value is family togetherness. I know that no matter what, my family will always be there for me. I didn't realize how important this was to me until I moved to N.C. I wasn't able to see my family all the time and it made me sad. I depend on them for so much.

*****

<u>Strategies for Generating Story Ideas</u>

Think of a person that matters to you. Write about stories connected to that person.

<u>Grandma</u>

-Disney World trip – Tower of terror, harmonica, fireworks

-giving me life advice

- yearly trip to Prospect Mountain

Mom

-Laying in grass watching her skydive or glaring at the stars

-Driving to Misquamiquette on 4th of July w/o reservations

-Trips / Camping

-Trying to find the Hollywood sign

-Winning Freihofer race

-Luggage searched in Amsterdam

- Ski accident

- Learning how to walk hills in Italy

Brian- teaching me to drive standard.

Katie & Courtney – Britney Spears lookalike contest

*****

Personal Narrative Writing – 10/14/14

Think of the first times, last times, or times you realized something. Write those stories.

1st Times

-Rollercoater

-Opening Christmas presents on Christmas Eve

-Decorating my house for Christmas

-Swam with dolphins

-ADK extreme

Last Times

-Drove my Tiburon to dealership to trade it in

-Haircut from someone I didn't know.

Times I realized something

-Found Aquarium in the bathtub

-Decided living in NY with family was more important than a job

-Science was not my "thing" and I'd never survive med school

-Be careful feeding horses through an electric fence

Personal Narrative Pre-Write

-16th birthday

-Trip to California

-Rent mustang

-Try to climb Hollywood sign

-Driving down coast

-Mom thinks Tijuana is close

-Wants real Mexican hot sauce

-Cross Border

-Can't see a town

-Missed the tourist town

-Park near car with no wheels

-Followed around town

-Run down town, people on street w/o limbs

-Food stand with fly's all over everything – people
eating

-Afraid car is gone

-Tijuana Story

*****

To the reader: There was a small box made of wood with a glass top that had an old picture of New York City and if I had to guess it was probably taken around 1950 or 1960 timeframe. A small latch on the side opened the box and inside are a bunch of small pieces of paper that look they were cut into the same size, perhaps from some pretty wrapping paper.

There was some writing on each of the pieces of paper in Erica's handwriting and the time frame for which she was writing these thoughts was very short. I remember when she told me that she was starting this new project, I was happy that I found it. She was thankful for her students, friends, and family – always her priorities. Here are some of her thoughts ...

March 17, 2015

St. Patrick's Day – I am grateful for my tutoring parents who trust me to help their kids improve and pay me well to do it.

March 18, 2015

I am grateful for Joe and Sunday being incredibly understanding of my crazy schedule – even when they need me and I can't be there.

March 19. 2015

My happy moment today was sharing Bob Dylan's "Times they are a changin'" and seeing a genuine understanding and appreciation in a usually disengaged group of 7th graders. I appreciate their willingness to be open to new things.

March 20, 2015

I am thankful for my mom for being so young and healthy and always helping to pull me out of a funk. I am excited to hang out with her tomorrow.

March 21, 2015

My moment of happiness was at a bar. And I got the attention of the best-looking guy there – a little like Matt. It pulled me out of my funk. I am grateful for my mom for getting me out of the house.

March 22, 2015

I am grateful for my ability to work out, my health, functional body parts, financial ability to pay for the gym and clothing. Not everyone has that. My happiness today was laughing hysterically with Liz at the gym.

March 23, 2015

I am grateful my mom lives so close and I have a place to go if/when I need too.

March 24, 2015

I am grateful for parents who trust me with their children's well- being and have confidence in my ability to positively impact their lives. I am grateful Dean is off drugs and committed to being healthy.

March 25, 2015

My happy moment was being able to overcome my anxiety – with the help of a smiling secretary. I am thankful for helpful caring people with genuinely good hearts.

March 26, 2015

I am thankful for a new teaching job in a place I love despite how the last one ended.

March 27, 2015

Dean came over and was the amazing wonderful man I love. My happiness.

March 29, 2015

I am grateful for Sally, bringing me on new fitness adventures and reminding me to try new things.

March 30, 2015

I am grateful for Danny and his generosity, especially when money is involved.

Marcy 31, 2015

I am grateful for the opportunity to experience things some never get to – like a $200 massage, a free trip to NC, and lunch at Mellow Mushroom.

April 1, 2015

I am grateful for my parents' health and their ability to be there for me – mostly mom – my biggest cheerleader.

April 3, 2015

My happy moment today was spending the night with bug … dinner, movie, drinks, snugs

Erica's Immunity Ninja Adventure

Hi! My name is Erica and this is the story of my immunity ninjas.

We are all born with immunity ninjas. They are the little warriors inside us, responsible for fighting off illness monsters and keeping us healthy. That's just their job, and they are good at it.

Sometimes, when an illness monster strikes, the ninjas are able to destroy the monster before we even know it is in us!

Other times, the immunity ninjas have to partake in a little battle inside our bodies. This is when we feel sick, like when we get a cold or an upset stomach.

Sometimes the illness monsters are really strong. This is when we get something a little bit worse than a cold or an upset stomach.

Once in a while, a really mean illness monster comes along. They are strong and evil, and sometimes our immunity ninjas are simply no match for this super-illness monster.

One of these super monsters decided to enter my body and start a battle with my immunity ninjas. This super monster was cancer, and my immunity ninjas needed a little help in the battle.

Fortunately, doctors have all sorts of medications and tools to help our immunity ninjas! My doctor gave me one kind of medication, called chemotherapy. There are lots of different kinds of chemotherapy. Some of them attack the illness monsters directly. It is like adding another army to help out your own ninjas in the battle.

Another kind of chemotherapy goes into your body and makes your immunity ninjas SUPER-strong. It's like giving your ninjas some super strong vitamins that boost up their muscles. This doesn't last forever, though. The ninjas need to get more medication to keep their strength up for the battle. So, people go to "treatment," where they get more medication.

Ideally, a person would get a few doses, or treatments, of chemotherapy. Their ninjas would fight the super monster battle, and then his or her body would go back to normal.

But life isn't *always* perfect, and medications aren't *always* perfect. Everyone's body is different, and everyone reacts to medications differently. When I got my first treatment, my immunity ninjas got superstrong and were able to fight the cancer monster. But the battle was not won yet. I knew I would need many more treatments. So, I went to the doctor and got my second treatment. But what happened next was something no one ever expected.

My immunity ninjas got their super vitamins and built their super-muscles. They continued to fight my cancer monster, and they seemed to be fighting a great battle! But then one day, I started to feel terrible.

After lots of x-rays and tests, the doctors figured out that my immunity ninjas actually got **too** strong! They got a little overexcited and forgot that they were only supposed to be fighting the cancer monster. They accidentally started attacking the healthy parts of my body too! They started attacking my lungs and other organs, and that is why I felt so horrible!

Since my ninjas were so strong, the doctors had to give me more medications to take away some of their strength and to calm them down a little. Unfortunately, just like a getting a cold or the flu, recovering from this battle takes time. My body had to repair itself and my immunity ninjas needed to get themselves back to normal too! All that fighting also made me very sleepy, so I had to take lots of naps.

Obviously, the kind of chemotherapy that I tried was not good for me. My immunity ninjas were not able to handle all of that extra strength. It's kind of like eating a bunch of candy and sugar and then trying to

sit still and read. It just doesn't work. But my doctors
were able to come up with another plan for me.
Everyone's immunity ninjas are different and may
need different kinds of chemotherapy to fight their
best. When one doesn't work, doctors can keep
trying to find the right one for our immunity ninjas
and help them win the battle and defeat the cancer
monster.

*Note to reader: Erica wrote this story to share
with her students. She felt it was important to
describe cancer in a way that would help
children understand what cancer is and how it
affects people without scaring them. Her thought
was that any parent, teacher, nurse, or anyone
could use this story to explain and open the
dialogue for a very difficult discussion.*

Passion is defined by Webster's Dictionary as "a strong liking or desire for or devotion to an activity, object, or concept." However, my passion is not a devotion to any activity, object, or concept. Rather, it is a combination and culmination of all of these. My passion stems from the devotion to the concepts of education, communication, and appreciation of differences amongst us. This manifests in my dedication to educating students of all ages, sharing my ever-growing knowledge and appreciation for culture, and practicing various forms of verbal, written, and expressive communication.

When I embarked on my post-secondary educational career, I, like many others, was not sure what it was that I wanted to do. I knew I wanted to work with people and experience the cultures of the world. I had already been to France and Italy and knew there was so much more that I had not seen. It was not until I was pondering the eloquent words of Emily Dickenson and becoming fully engulfed in my World Communication lectures that I realized that I wanted to explore both of these areas more fully. Stemming from my natural ability to relate to people as well as my appreciation for literature, I changed my major to education with a concentration in English. This proved to be a wise decision.

I spent the next 3 years in many classrooms, giving me the opportunity to add to the enrichment of hundreds of children's lives. Teaching English Language Arts to middle and high school students proved extremely rewarding as I helped those students develop their creativity in written and oral communication. However, my favorite lessons were always those in which I could share my cultural experiences in foreign countries. While an undergraduate student, I continued my study of the French language through my sophomore year. I have since often regretted discontinuing this course of study. I am excited for the opportunity to be immersed in the French culture including the language so that I can continue my path of fully understanding a culture other than my own.

I completed my Master's degree in literacy for birth to grade six. I firmly believe that literacy is a cornerstone of any culture. For those who struggle with reading and writing, the world can be a daunting and frustrating place. Communication falters. I knew that if I could help even one child become more literate, I would have achieved my goal. Fortunately, I was able to work with several children, increasing their literacy abilities and appreciation for written and spoken forms of communication.

I have most recently begun to work in a business setting, catering to customers from a vast array of countries. As I look around me, I realize that Global Communication is becoming more and more important in today's economy. Globalization is causing drastic changes in the way that we view the world and those around us. The internet and international media is changing how people communicate, interact, and even perceive various aspects of daily life. I want to explore this trend more fully. I want to understand the forces which drive us and the global economy.

I am now ready to more fully explore the cultures of the world. It is time for me to step outside of the comforts of home in order to more fully appreciate the customs, traditions, values, languages, and full cultures of the world. Traveling to Paris when I was fourteen years-old inspired my initial desire for these experiences. It is from the American University of Paris that I would like to continue my journey.

* * * * *

2011

We always received good certificates for the work Christmas party. It was pretty easy, really. I called other businesses, offered to trade their certificates or credit for nights in the hotel and voila- they arrived in the mail the next day. This job fell into my lap the year I took on the sales director position at the hotel. Retrieve certificates for the party. That party I was assigned- however, I courteously took it upon myself to sort these certificates by value and interest, and remove from the gift stack anything that I deemed better suited for my usage than a fellow employee. It was payment, I justified, for having to spend the excessive time locked in my office calling, bargaining, printing, signing, sending, receiving, and, of course, sorting. I had the right to whatever I wanted. Not without limit, of course. And lucky for the general manager, who happened to be one of my best friends and typically finds humor in my random acts of thievery, she got whatever I deemed better suited for her than other employees as well.

In past years, I had always ensured I had a weekend getaway in some New England hotel with a whirlpool suite. These were the good ones. Sure, the fireplace suite in the nearby sister property makes for a nice night out, but why bother when you can enjoy a whole weekend away from the mundane-ness of the capital district. This year, I decided to take a different route and contact some local restaurants. A hotel suite is valued around $120- which broke down to roughly 5 twenty-five dollar Friday's certificates. Two for me, two for her, one for the hotel. When considering the ration of work I do to what she does to what the rest of the employees do, it seemed fair. Okay, maybe I did spend eighty percent of my day cruising the internet and staring out the window, waiting for the owner to arrive so I could look busy. And sure, Chrissy spent hours working on her accounting homework (which, lucky for her, looked like she was working.) And the rest of the employees literally sweat and scrubbed and tucked and served. But our work was more important, and so, we deserved the night out, right? That's right, one hundred dollars in certificates. One night out. One long night out.

As I sat my fourth Mic-ultra bottle on the table of the booth we had now taken up residence in, I wondered aloud what to do from here. Chrissy was now joined by her husband, Vahan, and a mutual man friend, Nathan. We were collaboratively 14 beers deep and the night was young. Nathan was our designated driver- as in, he showed up and we designated him as the one to drive us home. Actually, we lured him here so that when he showed up we could designate him. So we were all equally amazed when he suggested a 3 hour drive to Canada for a little party time in Montreal. It wasn't so much amazement as interest in what could certainly be a memory-inducing, or erasing, adventure. And If it hasn't been for the excessive amount of alcohol buffered by the intense lack of food, I am not sure this idea would have ever progressed beyond that initial mention. But it did, and I soon found myself and Chrissy in the underwear section of Wal-Mart searching for a change of clothes to take and some pj's for the end of the night while the boys retrieved some cheap toothbrushes and shampoo. Is this really a good idea? I thought to myself. Chrissy was on call but had already found someone to cover for her. We didn't have a hotel but Vahan was on a mission to solve that. It all somehow just came together. Which was rare. Making plans with 4 people in 3 houses with vastly different schedules was not always possible, or even worth considering.

Much as this was not worth considering, we apparently also failed to consider the events that unfolded in the next three hours.

Approaching the border never seemed to concern anyone in the car. As Nathan rolled down the window, I am fairly certain a wave of stale beer-stenched air bellowed out and nearly knocked over the border patrol officer. Our driver was sober. We were in the clear. I cannot say the same for my vision or judgement, however. Because as I caught a glance of this officer, he looked quite familiar. Ridiculously unfriendly with a severe lack of emotional expression but nonetheless, familiar. And I thought he should know this. I also thought he should smile. I believe the conversation went a little like this:

Me: Hi!

Officer:

Me: You look really familiar.

Officer:

Me: Were you working on New Year's last year? During the day, when I came back home? I was driving. A black blazer.

Officer:

Me: Do you remember me? Were you working?

Officer:

Me: No.no, really, I'm serious. You must have been.

Officer: I was working ma'am.

Me: REALLY?! Wow, that's so weird!

Officer: Have a good night sir.

I'm not sure the laws governing this great nation, or Canada, for that matter. But I do know they do not tolerate public intoxication very well. And I am further certain that officer did me a great favor that day. Federal prison probably isn't pleasant- especially with a hangover.

The remainder of the night (as recounted to me) consisted of:

1. Walking around the corner just in time for last call at the local gay bar.

2. Kermit-on-Acid. Whatever the hell that is.

3. Paying the bar man $40 for a twelve-pack of open beer and an additional $20 to bring it to our room and ice it. Although apparently, we never got it.

And all I have to remember about this series of events is a photo of an alarm clock placed strategically on the side of my face where I passed out cold and toppled over. Maybe it was a lack of oxygen, Canada is higher than New York, right?

*****

<u>Why I selected teaching as a profession</u>. (May 2015)

When I was asked what I wanted to *be* in high school, I wasn't sure. But I did know what I wanted to *do*. I wanted to make a profound and positive impact on lives, my community, and the world. It sounds a bit cliché, but that was truly the most important thing to me.

I started this journey as a pre-medicine student at Siena College, ignoring my propensity for teaching and my natural ability to relate to, and understand children. I thought that solving the mystery of illness was the best way for me to be an asset to this world. It quickly became evident that I enjoyed helping my fellow students learn to study and prepare for their exams, then I did studying my own labs and books. My transition to education as a career, and subsequent transfer to Saint Rose, was one of the best decisions I ever made.

Teaching allows me to be creative, while positively impacting the lives of the students, families, and even colleagues around me. I love teaching. I guess in this way, I always knew what I wanted to *be*, rather than just what I wanted to do.

I have spent the majority of my teaching career in Suburban Council Schools. I understand the exceptionally high expectations of parents and administrators in these areas. I value this, as I also hold my students to the highest standards and encourage them to reach their maximum potential through the use of rigorous, relevant, and innovative lessons. Niskayuna CSD's Mission Statement begins with the word "empowered", that is exactly how I approach my teaching. I want my students to leave my room feeling like they can, and will, achieve anything they want to. My job is to empower them with the skills and abilities to make good choices and rise to the challenges that will lead them to success.

The Sexy Cop (college)

Halloween is one of those holidays that you love or hate. And you love or hate it for very distinct reasons. And those reasons change as you grow, change, and mature. When you are 18 and a freshman in college, your reasons are very specific. It is the one and only day of the year that it is perfectly acceptable to dress like you are preparing for a role-play session with a dominatrix in Vegas. It is the one and only time during the year that it is perfectly acceptable to wear hooker shoes, or cowboy boots, or no shoes at all. Because the worse you look, the more you are accepted and even celebrated for your daring originality and triumphant audacity. I am the Halloween queen. And that enthusiasm, I have learned, is infectious. So infectious, that I easily convinced the nearest 4 girls to join me in a Halloween night rendition of the Village- People. I, of course, would follow in Daddy's footsteps and become the cop. This would entail a simple black mini, half buttoned blue blouse, fishnets, knee boots, cop hat, handcuffs, and, of course, water gun. Because its only natural I would have a gun full of water to douse parched friends' mouths. Cassie, with her long, straight, dark brown hair would take on a Pocahontas persona, Kristin a biker, and little blonde Lindsay the sailor. That left Leah. Donned in her reflective orange vest (which fit her better than whatever construction worker she stole it from), denim mini (which looked more like crotchless underwear), yellow hardhat and topping off the ensemble with stiletto work boots (threatening to crumble under her weight at any moment), she was certainly a sight. We all were. But she brought a certain trashiness to the rest of us Catholic-college Brainiac's. She really ensured that we made a scene. That we were noticed for all the wrong reasons. But I suppose that was the point.

Leah was lucky, really, to have such a close friend with such incredibly exclusive party opportunities. She had decided against college and was living vicariously through my experiences. She had even become a semi-permanent resident on our sky-blue dorm rug, storing pajamas, pillow, and blanket under my bed. I didn't mind and Cassie never complained. We had fun. We had fun that Halloween night. Chasing shots in our dorm room with tap water and stolen juice led to a loud parade of the Village chics across campus- periodically stopping to laugh with the campus friars. Eventually we transverse the campus and found the campus townhouses- the senior housing. Hindsight, campus security would have been more efficient if they had simply prohibited underage underclassmen from entering the senior area. But they didn't. So we did.

*****

Paris Trip

It was the first day that we were expected to have rain. After being blessed with cloudless skies, it was time for the city to rehydrate. Fortunately, we were headed for one of the few indoor activities of interest to us in the City of Lights. Well, of interest to ME, Mom was a bit mortified by the thought of sightseeing thousands of bones assembled into artwork. And, in reality, we spent more time outside in line than we did in the Catacombs. Having read many trip advisor reviews, we knew that the lines were notoriously long. The Catacombs open at

10am, and most reviews suggested that we arrive early. We arrived at 9:25, and were shocked by the line that had already formed. The people in the front of the line were sitting in huddles on the sidewalk sharing snacks and comparing stories of their travels. To me, it looked more like the wee hours before the Black Friday sale at Walmart. I counted 225 people in front of us as we took our place in line. This number most certainly grew as families joined the person holding their spots in the line. Since they are only able to allow 200 people into the Catacombs at a time, and tour groups are allowed to skip the line, it was clear we were going to be here for a while. By the time we had made it to the point of seeing the entrance, the line behind us had wrapped clear around the entire city block, and my impatience had led me to begin making up stories to narrate the various wildlife around us. Once we entered the tiny structure which serves as an entrance, we paid our 10 Euros each and started down the loooong spiral staircase to the chilly Catacombs. And it was a long walk. Long enough to take out my phone and videotape the hypnotizing decent. Long enough for me to be dizzy and off-kilter when we reached the end. Which wasn't good, considering the ground is damp and very slippery. Ironically, mom did in fact slip once. But not to worry, she instinctively reached out and caught herself on a skull. Although when she realized what she and done, I think she would have preferred to fall.

Despite the many warnings that flashes are not allowed, we were able to snap some photos before being threatened by the light warden. And I actually think the photos I took on my iPhone without the flash came out better.

If you are into reading the plaques on the wall, and taking in some history, this might take you a little longer. But we are visual people and prefer to make up our own history behind the creepy stacking precision of the bones. We entered around 12:25, and were out in time to catch a lovely Italian lunch around the corner form the exit. We shared an antipasti salad (which was good when salt and pepper were added,) I had gnocchi, which was excellent, and Mom had smoked salmon linguini, which she loved, but I found a bit too fishy.

Whoever thought that it would be a good idea for two women to venture to the Port de Clignancourt flea market should be jailed for attempted manslaughter. This was by far one of the scariest, dirtiest places I have ever been (besides Tijuana). Upon reaching the top of the metro station staircase, we should have just turned around. But other reviews on TripAdvisor promised it was one of the greatest areas for shopping and that the antique area was second to none. We are two successful, educated, well-traveled women, who are used to navigating foreign countries, and we could not find one remotely useful or worthwhile item to purchase anywhere in sight. What we did find were hundreds of men selling stolen iPhone and knock-off sunglasses, cheap designed imitation clothing, and hundreds of other equally useless, potentially stolen pieces of rhinestone-embedded junk. When I refused to acknowledge a man selling fake ID's, he chose to step in front of me, blocking my way, before hitting me quite forcefully around my back. IT became obvious that I was being targeted for some reason and my 5'4" mother had to step

223

in and walk behind me, elbowing off intruders and acting as my maternal-instinct-fueled bodyguard. I didn't even feel safe when we were back in the metro station. That train could not move fast enough away from this disgusting, god-forsaken area.

The first time we attempted to visit the late Jim Morrison, where he was laid to rest in Pere Lachaisse cemetery, was a complete failure. Arriving at 6:08pm, our plans were shattered by the closed gates and tiny wilting sign declaring it had closed at 18:00. This after Mom worked all day and we traversed the city via 3 metro trains and 30 or so minutes. We thought we might redeem the remainder of the evening and wander the area, but we quickly realized this was not the most ideal place for us to spend our evening and walked until we found a more friendly shopping area. Much to our great relief, we were also able to locate a flat-shoe store, and not a minute too soon. 100 miles in flip flops cannot be good for anyone.

Melanoma (2016)

So, is this what my life has come to? 30 years old, lying in bed on a Saturday night at 9pm, googling "what should i bring with me to chemotherapy" and "when do side effects occur from Ipilimumab". Should I be out, enjoying time with friends, living it up, while I can? I'm tired. Am I tired because of the Cancer? Or just because I'm tired? Wait, let me google that: "Effects of cancer on the body" ... okay, obviously it causes cells to reproduce out of control. How about "effects of cancer on the body before treatment"? hmm... oh wait, this site says "fatigue" but it's not a reliable site. Whatever, someone out there must have cancer and feel fatigued too. It must be a real thing. I'm tired because I have cancer. Then why am I laying here, arm stretched across the bed to reach my phone, which I have already plugged in for the night? I should go to sleep, what time is it? 10:30?! How did that happen? I know I am going to wake up at the crack of dawn, why am I wasting valuable night hours?

This is why. As told through my "brave" Facebook post:

Some of you know what has been going on with me and have asked how it all started, and some of you have no idea. I'm not one to share this kind of thing on Facebook, but it was recently pointed out to me that sharing my story could help save a life, so here it goes (sorry it's so long, just read it) I had a tiny little freckle on my stomach for as long as I can remember. Over the last couple of years, it had grown some, eventually getting less symmetrical and even a little uneven colored (think brown tie-dye.) I ignored it for some time, but eventually I had it biopsied. Long story short, the biopsy came back that it was Malignant Melanoma (the deadliest skin cancer, often caused by sun exposure). And to make it worse, probably because I waited so long, it has even gotten into my lymph nodes. In just over 30 days, I have had 4 surgeries, resulting in 8 incisions (2 of which are over 3 inches long) and countless other tests, scans, and doctors appointments. I now need another surgery and 3 years of chemo. As horrible as this all is, it could have been even worse. If I had waited any longer, it could have spread to other organs, at which point it is almost impossible to treat. But I'll be ok, because I was proactive about it, and asked for a biopsy.

This absolutely is NOT to seek pity or attention, but rather to make people understand how deadly the sun can be without sunscreen with SPF and to recognize the symptoms before they get this far on you. I'm not a sun-worshiper, haven't been in a tanning bed in years, and I'm only 30 years old! If you even have the slightest doubt or question about something on your skin, please have it checked- sooner rather than later. Don't think or worry that you are being paranoid. A 5 minute body check and a little sunscreen could save you, and everyone who cares about you, a world of pain.

Alright, so there's a little more to it than that, but I guess if that is enough info for you, stop reading now and get on with your life. Just be sure to stop by a dermatologist on the way. If you are super nosy, overly concerned, or perhaps questioning your own prognosis-continue on. Though I make no apologies for hurt feelings (I can be a little snippy at times) or for oversharing. You chose to read it.

In 2010, I became a Beachbody coach - you know that company that creates the workout programs that fill the early-hours infomercial slots on TV? Well they also make this meal replacement shake, which I drank, and liked enough to continue drinking, and subsequently sell as a "Beachbody Coach" (which is not a pyramid scheme, but also way too complicated to attempt to explain here- even if I did understand it.) I lost some weight (be it from drinking the shake, or from the massive amount of working out I was doing, who knows.) But I won their monthly challenge and was paid $1000. It is worth mentioning that this all came about when I started dating an unemployed guy, trying to make it as a Beachbody coach. Though, if you have to sign your girlfriend up, just to make your monthly quota, I'd say it's fair to assume you might consider other money-making ventures.

The one thing this guy did have going for him was his natural, God-given 6, no 12-pack. He honestly spent 14 hours a day on the couch with a laptop surfing Facebook (work, he called it.) But never, ever worked out. Yet somehow, he had the body of a (short) Greek God! Anyway, when he applied to be a part of the filming of the new Insanity Infomercial, we brought it to the producer's attention that I, too, was in amazing shape and could be employed as part of the cast without having to pay for another hotel room in pricey Manhattan, near the filming studio.

So, for the next 2 years, I could be seen sweating and testifying as to the effectiveness of this program every day, around 2am, on all major network channels. A year later, I was again asked to star in one of their videos, this time in Las Vegas. I looked great in a bikini. Filming in the MGM Grand, they asked if I wanted a robe to walk from the makeup room to the filming area. I declined. I worked hard for that body. I wanted everyone to see it. My tiny freckles, spattering my body were not notable. They were just there.

I have looked back at those photos. I have zoomed in, trying to find any hint of what was coming. Trying to decide if any one freckle looked a little off. But nothing. None any large than if a pencil eraser were dipped in brown ink and stamped on my stomach. In fact, the one spot on my stomach actually felt like my very own Marilyn Monroe- inspired beauty mark.

The Beachbody Coach thing didn't really work for me, and neither did the guy who planned to make his millions selling Beachbody products. In fact, he didn't even make the cut for the infomercial. I continued on with my teaching career, relocating from Charlotte, where I had taken a year-long teaching job, out of desperation, back to Albany, NY. Five middle schools and countless dozens of prayers later, in August of 2015, my life was saved. And I mean that quite literally.

Having been bounced from job to job, my health insurance was never stable. I filled long-term leaves left open from sick or pregnant teachers. Some of these positions came with health insurance, some did not.

Regardless, the coverage ended with the end of the position. After filling one of these positions, I was given a permanent position in the school for the following year, including full health benefits. I had learned over the previous 5 or so years that I needed to take advantage of health benefits when I had them- squeezing annual OBGYN visits and teeth cleanings in as much as possible.

Now that I had a fairly permanent position (though nothing is really permanent when you are only part time,) I decided to finally get that pesky cyst removed off my ankle. It was harmless and benign, but I was sick of catching my razor on it and causing a scene reminiscent of the movie Psycho, every time I shaved in the shower. A dermatologist I had seen before for other, unrelated issues, removed the cyst and, upon request, checked the freckle on my stomach that seemed to be getting a little larger and even itched occasionally. He reassured me that it was nothing to be concerned about and sent me on my way. The only suggestion he had was to take pictures of it periodically and monitor for any changes. He didn't biopsy it. He didn't photograph it. He didn't suggest removal as a precaution. Sometimes I wonder if I shouldn't sue him.

As is my luck, the enrollment numbers for incoming 6th graders in the school district dropped by several hundred. And, perpetually occupying the bottom spot on the totem pole, I was the first to go. They no longer needed my part-time teaching services. But, I could choose to continue my health coverage for 18 months through the Cobra program. It would only cost me $650 per month. Now, this is something that is so perplexing to me. How, exactly, is one supposed to pay this sum of money for health coverage when they have been laid off and no longer have a source of income to draw from? That sum, $650 was more than half of what unemployment benefits paid per month, before taxes. But I didn't even qualify for unemployment. I was working a second part-time job at the time. Which, ironically, exempted me from being allowed to collect unemployment. I declined the Cobra coverage. It was easier, and cheaper, to pay for the occasional trip to the doctor and associated prescriptions out of pocket. Even if I got sick twice a month (which was my average) and was given antibiotics both times, it still only worked out to cost about $400 per month. And I was healthy otherwise, right?

I took the pictures. I monitored the "harmless" and "benign" freckle on my stomach. Even when the itching got worse. Even when it appeared to double in size. Even when, in the summer of 2015, I took my bathing suit cover-up off and my mother gasped "Erica, what in the hell is that?!? You need to get that checked!!" I still didn't see a doctor. Why? I was told by the dermatologist that it was harmless. Granted, that was a couple of years ago. But I am not one to be overly paranoid about these things. And really, did I have an extra $200 to go see a dermatologist, only to be told I was worried for no reason? After all, I didn't have insurance. What if it really was something to be concerned about? It had been there my whole life, it could wait.

I was working at the luxury car dealership, my second job-turned-primary job, when I was called for an interview at the job of my dreams. I attended and graduated from Shenendehowa. I got my first teaching job right out of college there. I would like to think I would have been a permanent employee there, had the recession of 2008 not gotten in the way. But I had a second chance. After a grueling, gut-wrenching, stressful couple of weeks, I learned that I was chosen as the best candidate for the position of middle school English teacher and I was offered the job, full health benefits included. I am not exaggerating when I say that I cried, a lot. After 8 years of uncertainty, my life could finally quiet down. My life could finally start. I could put down roots, make plans, live like a normal person. I was turning 30 the following November, and this was one of the more difficult items I listed on my "30-by-30" list. Check!

The 30-by-30 list was silly, really. But it gave me something to distract my mind from the inevitable. I was getting old. And I hadn't accomplished a lot of what I thought would be accomplished by this age. I always saw myself as a young mom. I thought I would be a tenured teacher with a gorgeous man, beautiful children, and a white picket fence. And up until I got that job, none of the above were even remotely near being fulfilled. I felt like my life was going to end at 30. Like, if I didn't have something to show for it, I was a failure in my own eyes. Perception is reality. I had to find a way around that. I figured, if I could accomplish everything on my list, I could move on to the next decade of my life with some semblance of control. The list turned out to be more difficult to tackle than I thought. In retrospect, I should have included goals with shorter timelines, like "work out with my best friend for a day" instead of "workout every day for 60 days" because really, those long-term things are hard to track. And missing one day meant resetting the counter, and I didn't have another 60 days before my birthday. Some of the goals were easy. Some of the things listed were things I did anyway. But there were a couple that I knew would really challenge me. Getting a teaching job was obviously one of these, and not entirely within my control, so that wasn't really fair. Thank God it worked out anyway.

Perhaps the only other really tough option on my list was to go skydiving. It was something I always wanted to do, but never seriously tried to plan. It wasn't something I wanted to do alone, and it is difficult to find a friend with the same ambition, who is also willing to dish out $300 for a 2-minute fall out of a plane. But that is why you have cousins. My cousins are more like sisters, and we all decided to make this a family affair. When we decided to jump, it was one of the last weekends of the season, but it was an unseasonably warm October. The day was amazing. I could go on for pages about the entire adventure. As my mom pulled into the gas station at the end of the day, refueling from the trip, I burst into tears. I was so overwhelmed by the love I felt that day. The fact that we all came together and pulled this day off. The fact that I had such an amazing group of people in my life. No one in the car understood what I was crying about. And I'm not sure I did either. But maybe I just knew. Knew that these would be the people I would lean on, be supported by, and thank God for over the next couple of months. Maybe that incredible intuition I have was telling me something.

I knew the freckle had to be looked at. I knew it from the size, the changing shape, the ragged edges, the uneven texture. I knew it from my mother's reaction. It had gotten so ugly that I no longer wanted to be in a bikini. It was almost embarrassing. But also knew that I would need stitches once I had it checked, and I wanted to skydive first. And then I wanted to enjoy my November birthday party. Then I would have it checked. Or at least ask my primary doctor what she thought.

1/26/16

Is this my new normal? Waking up, lying in bed, wide awake. Debating how badly I really need to pee, knowing that the pain would be excruciating. It is the first time since the surgery I did not wake up in 2-4 hour increments, re medicating with more Percocet, offsetting the rush of pain which would certainly flood my nerves, or what is left of the nerves, in my legs. Sure enough, the second my feet make contact with the plush carpet, and I am able to heave my body vertical, I feel it. Weight of fluid pulses down my legs and pushes out on my skin, pulses of pain, tightness, soreness. I keel over in agony. settling back on the bed until the initial pounding subsides. I know once I start my hobbling journey to bathroom, things will loosen up, or something. The pain will become less intense, more annoying. Within an hour, it will dull to aching, and disappear completely, as long as I am able to stay splayed out in the recliner.

But then there is peeing. My day would be easy if I didn't have to pee. I could skip eating and just stay in the chair all day. I mean, I even have the bottle of pain meds tucked in the cushion under my butt. Not that I am hiding them, it just seems to be a convenient location to keep track of all of accessories- remotes, computer mouse, pill bottle. If only I could tuck a magical pee fairy in there. A little creature that pops out, sucks out all of my pee, then disappears again. Is that weird?

I know I have to get up. Even if there was a pee fairy. I am supposed to walk around a little. Well, to be more precise, I am supposed to take a lap around the living room every time I pee. But what if I don't pee?

Is this my new normal?

Seven days since surgery. Still have stitches in my back (I hope 15 days is okay.) Three doctor's appointments tomorrow. No egg news yet. And my principal wants to know when he should plan to observe me. Where's the roll-my-eyes emoji when I need it?

The Port (2/9/16)

As much as she makes me completely insane sometimes, I am not sure how I would get through all of this without my mother. She is in Paris for work, so she couldn't bring me to surgery today. Thank God I have an amazing family, because my friends are all but useless when it comes to getting rides. Deanne is having baby issues, so she gets a pass. Liz said it was too short of notice to get the day off. Andreya took days off last week, which I guess means she can't take a day off this week. And Cher has way too many kids to have deal with taking care of me too. So, Aunt Terri will bring me. I guess it was only a matter of time before the surgeries and needing a ride started to add up. This is what, surgery 4? 5? I don't even know anymore.

We were late getting to the hospital, 15 minutes, partially because I didn't account for rush hour, and partially because it snowed and the roads were terrible. One way not to go into surgery is to have the front desk guy hassle you about being late, disregarding any excuses, as everyone else got there on time. I'm not even really sure what he was doing at the registration desk, he is just the tech who pushes beds around. And not that anyone was in any real hurry to get me into surgery, we ended up in the waiting area for another 15 minutes. Thankfully, once I was checked in, things moved a little quicker. The nurse who came to do my IV and ask me 358 questions was very sweet. She was a cancer survivor and understood the annoyance and pain of having difficult veins. She took her time and nailed it on the first try. Then she left me with some advice- never tell a nurse your veins are hard to find because then they get nervous and miss. Good to know.

I was brought down to the holding area for surgery, and in time realized (and was later told) my surgeon was running a little behind with her previous patient. Thank God I was in the middle of the room and was afforded some entertainment or that 2 hours would have taken forever to pass. It really was a bit of a soap opera in there. One man was very angry that the doctors didn't want to operate on him because his blood sugar was dangerously high. He was taking his frustrations out on them, ignoring the fact that he was near death and surgery would almost guarantee he would not wake up.

Despite their recommendations that he call his primary doctor immediately, he refused, continued to argue, and eventually got dressed and left with his wife. His stubbornness is most certainly going to kill him, if his blood sugar doesn't kill him first.

I also learned that the incredibly fit woman beside me had been brought in the day before due to persistent vomiting and nausea. The girl to my left was in miserable pain from some kind of stones in her kidneys or urinary issue. This was actually one of the more entertaining cases, as she was still terribly uncomfortable after the procedure, writhing around on the bed. the nurses decided to let her anesthesia lull her back to sleep for a while. I can't say I blame them.

By the time I got home, I was acutely aware that I would not be going to school the next day, and that I was also going to have a very long time of painful unrest ahead of me. Terri went to get me dinner and my meds, and my friend David came over. While this guy had been an amazingly understanding individual up to this point, I am not sure that he was prepared for all of this. I am not sure I was prepared for him to witness all of this. As I was preparing my nightly cocktail of IVF meds to be injected, I got incredibly dizzy. My face got red, I got very dizzy, and he had to help me over to the chair in the living room. I suppose this is why they insist someone stay with you the day of anesthesia. I was able to regain my composure, but he had to finish mixing up my meds for me. He, of course, was traumatized.

Another one bites the dust (2/10/16)

I knew something was up last night. I could feel it in the way he was pulling away from me. The way he didn't snuggle back. The way he answered my texts when I asked if he wanted to have dinner together last night. But when he left, it was obvious something was wrong. I asked and asked and he lied and lied. He told me it was all okay, he was okay, we were okay. Until I texted him. Which went exactly like this:

Me: Are you sure we're ok?

Him: idk

Me: What's the matter????? :(

Him: Just everything

Me: I don't know what to say. I'm sorry.

Him: Don't be sorry.

Me: I knew this was going to happen. I should have known you were too good to be true. That's why I asked you so many times if u were sure u were okay with it. But I guess yesterday made it real for you. I'm not gonna lie, I'm crushed. But there's nothing I can do. I didn't ask for any of this. Good luck I guess. I hope you find a girl you deserve.

Him: It's not like that, I think it's just too much too fast

Me: I asked you that last night and you said no. Why all of a sudden? Something happened. You were 100% with me before…

Him: idk

Me: Well I'm not going to be made to feel bad for something I can't control. Or for having feelings that up until yesterday you were reciprocating. U literally have broken my heart.

Him: :(:(:(:(

So did I end it or did he? Was he getting ready to end it anyway? Am I mad? Who does this to someone with Cancer when they know about it and willingly enter into

that world? What happened? Was it his ex? I knew I
shouldn't be dating. I really liked him. A lot. Damnit.

2/12/16

Still no word.

It is the day before February break. I have been
back to school for two days, but my mind is anywhere
but there. I can't even focus on a lesson. It takes all I
have just to get through watching the kids for their 10
minutes of required reading at the start of every class. I
check my phone every 10 minutes, hoping for a text
from David, and there is never anything there. My job
has become to be my own personal secretary, chasing
down doctors notes and appointments, ensuring I have
sub plans and absence forms signed. I am thinking a
week ahead of myself constantly, because there is no
other option. The last thing I want to do is demonstrate
my keen teaching abilities for an observation that will
count for 30% of my APPR score. But, hey, why not. I
just wanted it to be over. I just wanted to have the
evidence that I am a good teacher, despite what is going

on in my personal life. And now, I am glad it is over. I guess it went well. He seemed pleased. He told me I did really really good. He has to. I'm sick. People have to be nice. Well, apparently not David.

2/13/16

Today is Saturday. I am curled up in a ball in the corner of my couch. Not because I have to. but because it is the only place I want to be. My port area is almost healed, and I am finally able to use that arm a little more, though it is still sore. My heart is more hurt than any part of my body at this point. I tried to trick David into talking to me by telling him I had a package coming to him but I canceled it, but just in case it came. He was mad. I thought he was mad because he was afraid Ashley (his ex) would find it before he did. But Cher pointed out that he is probably just mad at me. I did break up with him, after all. I wasn't getting very far with that discussion, so I ignored Liz's advice and sent him a very honest, very heartfelt long note telling him exactly how I feel and asking what I did wrong. I'm not begging for another chance, but I guess it is better to know what I did

245

wrong, so I don't do it again, right? I know I have completely lost it. I mean, we dated for a week! But for some reason, I just can't get past this one. I actually let tears trickle down my cheek today, for him. For the loss of him. For the loss of myself for the next 3 years. For another 3 lonely Valentine's Days.

There are things I really should be worried about besides my one-week boyfriend about whom I cannot stop obsessing. I am supposed to do my "trigger" shot tonight to have my eggs retrieved on Monday. The problem is, there are no testing locations open on Sunday, and therefore no way to tell if the trigger shot worked or not. So now, we have three options. 1- Someone comes in tomorrow just to do my test, but this means turning on the machine just for one person, which is apparently a huge issue. 2- Someone can come in at 5am on Monday to do my test and send me over to Waltham (3 hours away) for the retrieval if everything is okay. Or 3- I just go to Waltham and hope everything is okay. If it isn't, they send me home to return 2 days later and try again. That last option is probably the worst, although they say the chances it won't work are slim to none. But it isn't up to me. All I can do is sit and wait until someone calls me and tells me the plan. Story of my life.

2/16/16

Its pouring rain. Which is better than snow, I guess. I'm not exactly in great shape to be brushing off my car this year. We have only had a total of 5 inches of snow or so. I am pretty sure God did that on purpose. There's no way I could have gotten myself to all of these appointments in any worse weather. And today, I actually don't mind the rain. While I don't need an excuse to be lazy and lay around on the couch all day, it makes me feel better about making the choice to do just that.

Mom and I drove out to my sister-cousin Julia's house near Boston Sunday night. It was only 40 minutes from the IVF facility, where I was having my retrieval done, so it was easier than driving at 5am. They decided to just start the retrieval process without doing a blood test first, since we never were able to find an open clinic. The office itself was very nice, very modern. The holding area before surgery was super clean, and the curtains were spackled with multicolor circles. They had me change and then await surgery in a green plastic recliner, instead of a hospital bed. That was nice, I guess. It made the whole thing seem less like a surgery, and more like a minor procedure. And the nurses were incredibly sweet. The first one had the cutest haircut and smile. Her features made her look like a movie star or something. She kind of had that face that looked like you have seen her somewhere before. The post-op nurse was also very nice. She put my IV in before the procedure, and made sure to take her time finding my vein for the IV. I wish I could say the same for the anesthesiologist. His name was Vladamir, or some other very Russian name. He was very formal, brusque, everything one expects of a Russian. But, he knocked me out and woke me up, so I suppose he did his job.

I was a little confused when they had me walk into the operating room. That was a first. Especially because I was in socks and all I could think of were the lawsuits they might have should someone accidentally step foot on a dropped needle. The operating room was exactly as one would expect. They had me climb up onto the bed and wedging my butt cheeks into a little cutout at the base. But when they attached two bright orange poles to each side of me, and had me place my feet in the swinging stirrups, that was a bit unnerving. I began telling the nurses that if that is anything like having a C-section, I never wanted to have kids. Clearly, one would not have their legs in stirrups by their ears for that kind of procedure, but I was drugged. And then I passed out.

When I woke up, I was a bit uncomfortable. After 5 or so surgeries, I have come to understand that they will give me the entire syringe of pain meds, if I am above a 4 on the pain scale. So, I do not go below a 4 until the entire syringe is gone. There is absolutely no point in suffering through anything. If they can make me pain free and happy, I have no reason to refuse! So, drugged up and sucked dry of eggs, we got back in the car and headed home, 2 or so hours later, they had retrieved 16 eggs and sent me on my way. Later lab results showed only 13 of them were mature, which they need to be for use. Apparently, that is a good yield. Go me!

So, now I have been between the couch and bed for the past 28 hours. I have alternated between stool softeners, Percocet, and random trips to the fridge. My boobs are swollen and I feel like I have been constipated for weeks. Not sure if those are side effects, but I can only imagine a sudden drop in hormones would do that to a person.

Saturday also meant a small breakthrough in the David case. He finally answered my epically long text begging for some explanation of his sudden disappearance and what I did wrong. He claims that he just isn't ready and that there is nothing I did wrong. He thinks its crazy that I don't hate him. It is pretty obvious to me that he is having a hard time letting go of his ex. Which is fine. I was starting to get over him anyway, but I am glad that I know it wasn't me. Or at least that's what he said. I offered to be there as a friend and he couldn't understand why I'd do that. I texted him yesterday, 25 hours ago, asked how he was. He has not answered. Guess he doesn't want to be friends.

*****

Sam,

I am the oldest in the family of cousins, and obviously an only child. When I went off to college, I didn't really have anyone to talk to about the road that lay ahead of me as I started that first year at Siena. You are in the same boat – you are the oldest of the cousins (not yet already of college, etc). And you are the older sibling. So, take this with a grain of salt, but here are my wonderful words of wisdom. I haven't steered you wrong, yet, right?

1. Live on campus. At least until Junior year. You have no idea how much you miss if you aren't there – random impromptu games in the common areas at midnight or hikes to the food hall together – hungover in solitude.

2. No working freshman year. And if you decide to work after that, limit your hours, and work on campus. Try for somewhere cool, where your friends can stop by – like a sub shop or something. The money isn't worth missing out on the memories you would be missing – or your grades suffering. You need time for both.

3. Don't date. At least not freshman year. You need to experience college, find your place on your own before you start trying to fit someone else in. You are only a freshman once. Don't miss out on the time when everyone is new and making new friends.

4. Limit the hearts you break. I'm going to keep this short and sweet. Before doing anything with any girl,

ask yourself the following: Is she drunk? Does she think this is going to turn into a relationship that I don't want? Does she smell funny? If you answered yes to any of those, umm, RUN!

5. Get involved. Join some clubs, do something cool maybe Student Events Board or something. You get to meet the famous people who come to campus. You make friends outside your normal circle. And the connections you make now will help you in the future.

6. Be nice. This isn't high school anymore and everyone will realize that soon enough. Be nice to the guy that obviously hasn't ever been to a party, invite him. Hold the door for your professors. No, hold the door for everyone. And apologizing when you are wrong. No matter the circumstance. You never know when or where you will meet those people again.

7. Finally – get close to a professor. Find a professor you like, one who likes you and keep in touch with him/her. Ask advice, check in. You are going to need recommendations and references from college professors when you graduate. You better make sure at least one knows you.

I hope this helps – and as always I am here for you ..Er

Note to readers …

Erica Lynn Ladu lost her battle with Melanoma cancer January 26, 2017. She was strong for everyone right up to the very end. Her family was by her side supporting her all the way. Although she tried as hard as she could to fight the cancer, there was another plan for her.

I truly believe that God sent down this angel to teach us and work with his children to ensure they learned the tools they need in life as well as be a strong role model for all to be successful. He obviously felt her time on earth and her mission was complete – he took her home … she is now one of his beautiful angels amongst us all.

I know she is happily reunited with all those gone before her and they were there to guide her home when her time was ready. I'm pretty sure she grabbed Gizmo at the Rainbow bridge on her way up!

Although we have lost a beautiful, strong, smart, silly, devoted, caring and determined person in our circles – I look forward to seeing her again … and I know I will… Mom

Text: Erica to Mom – January 11, 2017

"Mom, relax. We're gonna fix this. And if we don't, we don't. I love you. Put comfy clothes on and get ready for another adventure!!"

Safely Home *(Prayer found in Erica's treasures)*

I am home in Heaven, dear ones;
Oh, so happy and so bright!
There is perfect joy and beauty
In this everlasting light.

All the pain and grief is over,
Every restless tossing passed;
I am now at peace forever,
Safely home in Heaven at last.

Did you wonder I so calmly
Trod the valley of the shade?
Oh! But Jesus' love illuminated
Every dark and fearful glade.

And He came Himself to meet me
In that way so hard to tread;
And with Jesus' arm to lean on,
Could I have one doubt or dread?

Then you must not grieve so sorely,
For I love you dearly still:
Try to look beyond earth's shadows,
Pray to trust our Father's Will.

There is work still waiting for you,
So you must not idly stand,
Do it now, while life remaineth –
You shall rest in Jesus' land.

When that work is all completed,
He will gently call you Home:
Oh, the rapture of that meeting,
Oh, the job to see you come!

As I Sit in Heaven *(found on Erica's phone)*

As I sit in heaven
And watch you everyday
I try to let you know with signs
I never went away
I hear you when you're laughing
And watch you as you sleep
I even place my arms around you
To calm you as you weep
I see you wish the days away
Begging to have me home
So I'll try to send you signs
So you know you are not alone
Don't feel guilty that you have
Life that was denied to me
Heaven is truly beautiful
Just you wait and see
So live your life, laugh again
Enjoy yourself, be free
Then I'll know with every breath you take
You'll be taking one for me …

71478802R00154

Made in the USA
Middletown, DE
24 April 2018